THE DEAD SHALL RISE

ZOMBIE, ZOMBIE, ZOMBIE

JAY WILBURN, ARMAND ROSAMILIA, AND ERIN LOUIS

Book 10 in Crystal Lake's Dark Tide series

Let the world know:
#IGotMyCLPBook!

Crystal Lake Publishing
www.CrystalLakePub.com

WELCOME
TO ANOTHER

CRYSTAL LAKE PUBLISHING
CREATION

Join today at www.crystallakepub.com & www.patreon.com/CLP

Subscribe to Crystal Lake Publishing's Dark Tide series for updates, specials, behind-the-scenes content, and a special selection of bonus stories
- http://eepurl.com/hKVGkr

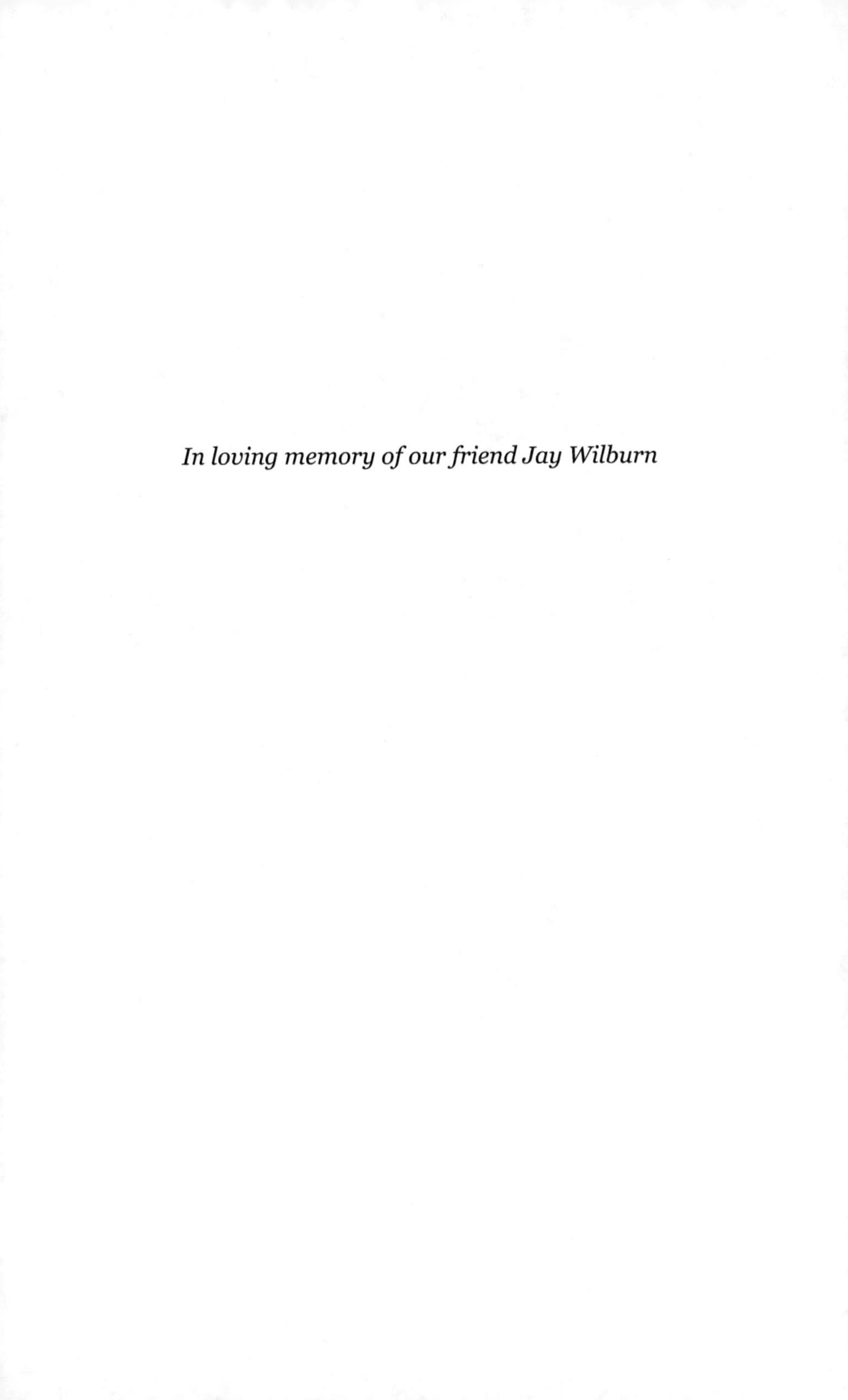

In loving memory of our friend Jay Wilburn

PREPARE BECAUSE DEATH IS COMING

JAY WILBURN

1

I WAS THERE when the messenger died on the edge of our territory, out by the green highway sign that read *Dry Stretch* in a language none of us spoke or read any longer. My dad was there to see and hear it too. So was Ethic Hanover, who was the loudest voice in favor of taking the messenger's story seriously. My mother showed up later, hustling me and my brothers away before I could hear all of it. Eventually, all of Dry Stretch would be gathered to discuss it.

The messenger was chewed up good, like the stories of what it was like when the undead were everywhere and humankind was on the brink of extinction, the way the traveling evangelists talked of it in church revivals. His clothes were torn. Blood around his crescent wounds dried black and gummy. The puncture points of the dull teeth (because zombie teeth are our teeth), of course, were swelled up; angry and red around the edges with pink rivulets of blood infection worming out from the festering bites. The poor bastard was hot with the fever of it, just like in the old days before my time, before my dad's time; back before most people younger than Granby could remember, except from the tellings. His open sores wept green and slimy off his pallid skin and into poisonous mud in the dust of our road.

I thought he was babbling deliriously at first because he stuttered so much before he got the first real words out from where he curled on his side, squinting up between the three of us into the sun. "The zombies, a horde as broad as the horizon, sweeps the land and comes this way to fell all before it. Prepare, for they come for you all. Bear me witness."

"Nonsense," my father breathed out, denying him witness instead.

"Bay," Ethic said without looking up from the infected dying man. No more reproach than that, just my father's name said evenly. Could have been reproach or a substitute for shut up. Could have been shock at my father's quick and dismissive response despite the evidence before our eyes. My father had used the uttering of my name on countless occasions for countless meanings.

My dad glared at the side of Ethic's face for a goodly count of time, a face he'd whisper against soon.

Ethic was younger than my father, but both were highly respected in town. My father had produced four children all by my mom, and all boys, like some repeating miracle. King, Kip, and Knoll were five, six, and eight in that order. Then, I was the oldest. Our farm barely produced enough to feed us all and to sell a little off the top of what was stored. But boys were worth more than all the acres put together. My father didn't think that way about us even though each of us had proposals on the table from the fathers of daughters all across Dry Stretch and beyond with healthy doweries in offer.

Ethic was something different. As I've gotten older, I understand he was a necessary thing in modern times with modern problems, but necessity comes at a cost. Ethic wasn't married, but being male and fertile, he was called upon to lie with the wives of other men that they might father children. He did so successfully too and was paid for it to boot. As far as I knew and as far as I saw at my age, he never attempted to repeat his performances without being asked by the husbands and never tried to claim the children he planted in other men's fields.

My father never had need for those particular services of Ethic or others like him. My father had offers of his own to plant in other fields but never took up on it. Still, husbands tended to look on Ethic with a level of disdain and mistrust. That was the cost and might be partly why Ethic had such trouble trying to convince my father and others to believe the message even though Ethic Hanover had traveled far into the wide world with his other work.

From the ground, the messenger held out a folded bit of paper with a poor wax seal barely holding the flap. It was frayed around the edges, discolored, and stained. The man was missing two fingers above the middle knuckles on the hand holding the paper. I don't know if that accounted for the stains, but they were poorly clotted and never going to heal.

He said, "Take this and bear the warning. I've completed my last mission and ask for final mercies from you to spare me the . . . Sir?"

The messenger held the note out to my father, but he backed up a step. My father was the oldest present and therefore held authority on taking the message.

"Sir, please, time runs short." He waved the paper almost as if he intended to toss it. My father backed up another step, placing one hand on the leather of his gun holster at his hip and the other firmly on my shoulder. Again, I wasn't best at reading signals, but I thought maybe my father feared I might go take the paper in his stead. I was that sort of kid, I suppose.

The messenger gave a frustrated huff and sized up my father with his eyes glazing over and his head cocked nearly upside-down against the dirt. A little pink spittle bubbled from the corner of his mouth.

He rolled toward Ethic next and recited through to the end this time. "Take this and bear the warning. I've completed my last mission and ask for final mercies from you to spare me the indignity of becoming one of them upon death. Grant me final mercies, please, sirs."

Ethic took the sealed letter between two fingers, and the messenger's arm dropped limp to the ground. His eyes rolled to the whites laced with the blood of broken vessels within.

Ethic poised his thumbnail against the wax seal and glanced over at my father, "Bear me witness, Bay?"

"I do." My father released my shoulder and drew his gun, holding it down by his other side for the time being.

Ethic broke the seal and unfolded the abused page. He read it through with only the harsh breathing of the messenger to punctuate it. He offered it to my father who shook him off.

My mother arrived and shouted at my brothers to return to the house. She called me to come even as she stepped into the roadway and forced me along with her bodily. I'd borne witness up until then. I felt I had a right.

Before I could say so, my father growled, "Go with your mother, boy. This day has enough trouble without you adding to it."

She marched the four of us across the field and away from what I thought to be the most interesting moment in my life.

I barely heard the page rattle when Ethic said, "We need to call a full body. We need the mayor to preside. Will you back me on that?"

"Of course," my father said as if insulted.

"Sirs, please."

I tried to turn my head, but my mother locked onto my sun-scorched neck with an iron claw, forcing me hunched and forward.

I heard the hammer on my father's gun click back. Should have been too far to hear it like that even on a clear day. But like a father clicking his tongue in church, should you dare mischief, I was prone to hear my father's clicks clearer than most.

"Will you bear me witness?" my father asked.

"This man needs and asked for final mercies," Ethic declared. "I bear you witness."

My father's shot ripped through the day and startled us all, even those of us who knew it was coming. My mother cleared her throat as she held firm to me, and the roar still echoed across the fields. Kip gave out a little cry of surprise, and King started weeping outright.

The messenger stopped his begging because his work was done, and final mercies had been administered. Though infected, he would never turn zombie to rise again hungry and deadly. The next thing was the handling and burning of the tainted flesh. After that was the full body gathering in the town hall.

2

In the center of the town square, at an angle to the hall where my father took me with him for the full body, was another mounted green sign from an ancient highway, like the one that still stood natural out on the edge of our territory, at the corner of our furthest field, the spot where the messenger arrived and expired before he could see all the turmoil he inspired across Dry Stretch. That green sign, the one mounted in town, had fewer holes in it. Fewer than the one near our land and far fewer holes than the fences and walls around town. Not good for a possible oncoming horde, but Dry Stretch had forty years or more to grow used to the world as it was becoming and not as it used to be.

My father and I filed in with all the others and took a spot in the middle right of the hall, near an aisle so we could exit quickly when the time came, same as we did in church, although the sanctuary of our church was smaller than this. Mom didn't come with us and neither did my brothers. My father and I were enough to represent the full body for our family.

Granby, my mother's grandfather and my great, came on his own. He lived in the farmhouse with us. We could have represented on his behalf as the head of house and heir. At first, he'd said he didn't want to come on account of his gout flaring and didn't ride with us. Then, he'd strapped up a buggy and came anyhow, gout or no. My father probably wished later he hadn't, but 'twas probably right he was there as there were few people left who could remember how it used to be.

The rest of the hall filled in with the representatives or full families for the meeting. It got stuffy in there quick, which would only add to the heated mood.

Ethic was there and sat up close to the front.

Even with a lot of the reps being the men of the families, the women in the hall still outnumbered the men more than four to one. The total population of the town, including the young children and the few babies, was probably closer to five to one. That was the way of the world.

The mayor at the time was Jetty. She ran quite a ranch. If not the most acres owned by a person in Dry Stretch, then close to it, and animals to spare. She was barren but married to a widower named Half who'd fathered a dozen daughters, none of whom lived with him.

She bore that stained paper and told the circumstances by which we'd come about it. She asked Ethic for a witness to her telling, and he gave it from the floor. She then testified it had been sealed when received by the infected messenger. She asked to be borne witness again. Ethic gave it and my father backed him, having witnessed the seal before Ethic broke it.

I couldn't help myself and cried, "Me too."

Chuckles spread through the room at that.

My father did not chuckle. He squeezed my shoulder hard and muttered my name. I got the message that he preferred I bear my witness in silence for now.

Mayor Jetty read the note.

"The written message reads, 'We may be the last survivors of Brady Hollow. As such, we send these messages in all directions to warn against the fate that befell us. We especially send them south to warn those in the path of the zombie horde.'"

A young woman, Liberty her name was, barren also and hired out to work the larger ranches and farms on a rotating basis, asked, "Where's Brady Hollow?"

Aleo, not much older than me but a proper landowner with the deaths of her parents, called out, "North of here. We're south of them."

Wasn't known if Aleo was barren. Hadn't come up yet. Of course, now we know.

Grumbles passed through the hall, but Jetty raised her voice and continued, "The numbers are vast. We fought hard once we realized what we were up against, but we realized too late. We'd seen more zombies coming in from the reaches and ruins, more than usual. We noted they were more lively so to speak, than the dregs we've tended to run across in recent years, but we did not think to prepare. Our fences and walls were in ill repair. We confess that we scavenged some sections of them for other purposes, leaving us wide open to attack, especially from a horde such as this."

Yellow, a farmer on a river plot as far south as we were north, called out from her seat in the back, "Our fences are in ill repair."

More grumbles.

Locust called out from her corner of the room. She was a craftsman in both wood and metal. She knew chemicals too. Skilled and respected, she was. She'd be the one to maintain the fences and walls if the town had called for it, which was probably why she felt the need to respond. "No one has thought it important to maintain the fences and walls. I've offered more than a hundred times over the years, but not a vote for it, I remember, and no benefactors stepped up to fund it, even at a discount."

"Stop interrupting the mayor like a bunch toddling young'uns hungry for the tit," Glorigold shouted from front and center off to Ethic's left. She was a rancher of note. Her piece was mostly across the river, but on both sides and she was still considered part of Dry Stretch. Raised both cattle and sheep from her youth, and she was old then, not near as old as Granby, but still an elder. Was considered weird business to mix sheep and cattle. One type of rancher tended to look down on the other on account of how each type of animal interfered with the grazing of the other. No one knew what to make of her, but she had age and wealth, so opinions didn't matter much.

Zink—not as young as Locust or Yellow, certainly not Aleo, but not as old as Glorigold either—scolded, "Don't be profane in full body, please."

Zink was acting preacher in the main town church at the time, ever since the last man to hold the job had gone home to be with the Father after his heart burst in the middle of a sermon on God's anger with sinners. She still ran her farm near town during the week. It was no big production in comparison, but she took care of herself and never really preached on tithing, so people showed her deference.

"Respect, Zink, but this is not your sanctuary," Glorigold said back.

"Respect, but there are young children present both places." Zink pointed out.

I took the moment of back and forth to lean to my father and ask, "We're on the northern end of Dry Stretch. Does that mean the horde would come through us first?"

"Hush," my father said. "We don't know anything of the sort yet. Quiet and listen."

Mr. Half interrupted the hall at that point, standing to say, "We haven't even heard the whole message yet. Let's keep order that long at least."

The grumbles around the hall were the agreeing sort then. The crosstalk died out then.

As Half sat back down, his wife, the mayor, glared at him. I saw it. I'm sure others did too, but I didn't understand it at the time. Seemed to me he was helping, and the full body seemed to agree. What I've learned since is that men always think they're helping, and they tend to think highly of their help no matter how outnumbered they are by the woman shouldering most of the weight of things. Aleo's told me that many times.

Jetty said, "The message continues. 'They overran us. At the height, it was like the Earth vanished and only the bodies of the dead filled the universe shoulder to shoulder and off into forever. We lost many. Most perished. We're still hemmed in and the messengers run the gauntlet to deliver these messages at their peril. If you good people hear nothing else, hear, understand, and heed this: Prepare, for death is coming like it has not been seen since the fall of the first days.' We bear witness."

A cacophony of voices rose up.

Jetty added, "I do not recognize the names of all the elders of Brady Hollow, but I see the mayor's script and bear witness myself the name is correct, and his scrawl matches."

No voices then. The pews creaked and popped with nervous motion though.

Liberty asked, "How far north is Brady Hollow?"

Aleo answered her again. "A touch over 25 miles."

"Long way for a messenger to run in one go," someone noted.

Aleo added, "Portmire and Silence Bay lie between us and them in that order running the river southward. Silence is still eighteen miles north by northwest."

"Haven't heard from any of them in a while," Locust said.

"What does that mean?" someone almost groaned.

"Let her speak," said another.

Locust looked about and stood as if being granted the floor properly. "I trade north and south along the river as do many here. I testify that I have not heard regular communication or the usual trade traffic by land or water for an unusual number of cycles. Nothing from Silence Bay, Portmire, Brady, or points north."

Voices competed. It was Half who tried to help again. "Can anyone bear witness?"

Things quieted down. Aleo stood as Locust sat. "I bear witness. I don't do as much business north as I do to closer points south like Hallifax or Nye Fate, but there has been no travel or word from the north in an unusual amount of time. It's enough that I almost inquired."

The hall erupted at that point.

Jetty finally banged the gavel. It took a bit, but people trailed off. She asked, "Ethic, you patrol the wider reaches near the ruins between us and points north. Have you seen any of the changes the message speaks of, in the behavior of the dead, I mean?"

Ethic stood and turned to the crowd. He had only just inhaled to speak when the interruptions began again.

Liberty first. "Should we send word south to Nye Fate and beyond, pass on the message the messenger gave his life to deliver?"

"Seems we should send a party north to investigate the quiet that has befallen."

"That's where the dead are!"

"We don't know that!" Glorigold shouted louder than the rest, but it didn't have nearly the impact of the gavel a moment ago.

"We have to send someone. I say Ethic. He can do it."

"Will need to be more than him, if any of this could be true."

"I nominate Ethic."

"Second."

Jetty banged her gavel. "The floor isn't open to motions or nominations of any sort yet. The full body will come to order, so we can discuss this. We need to get our heads around this situation before we can run off making suggestions. I know this is heavy business, true or not, and that is why we have the full body present. But we get nowhere if you can't talk through the details before we argue them or panic over them. Bear me witness."

"Hear! Hear!" passed through the hall with vigor. "I do" and "I so witness" were scattered in there too.

Ethic was still standing when Jetty said, "You have the floor Ethic Hanover."

That was when Granby stood. He was seated a little forward from where we were, closer to the front. Whether he did that for honor or because of his hearing, that's where he was. My father stiffened enough for me to feel it at my shoulder, and I was afraid.

Granby said, "Will you yield the floor for a brief word from an old man, Ethic if I promise to keep it short and hand it back promptly?"

Ethic nodded and spoke as he was taking his seat again. "I yield the floor to you, Granby."

So, Granby turned toward the bulk of the crowd gathered in that stuffy hall. He managed to limp as he did it even though he was only turning in place. And he spoke.

3

My father and Ethic stood over the zombie flailing weakly in the ditch out near our fence line. As they spoke and debated much like they had done in the hall before the full body the day before, I remember wondering if that mere fence would keep out a horde as well as it kept our few animals in.

"This is the state of these pests," my father said.

Ethic glanced down at the lone creature. Its jaws opened wider, but never really closed all the way again. Missing teeth and showing black sockets in its gums, the hard skin of its cheeks was split down to strings that hardly stretched when the jaws opened. One eye cocked up and away, unmoving, making the dead man look stupid. The other pupil was pinned and almost looked squared off as it rolled from my dad to Ethic and occasionally to me.

Ethic looked out toward the road where we'd come upon the messenger who set this whole controversy in motion. "This isn't how it is everywhere, Bay."

"I heard your word on it," my dad said. "I respect you and the work you do, but that does not make some fabled horde true."

"Something set against the people of Brady Hollow. Something silenced traffic from the towns north."

"Could be many things, but I can't look on this pitiful creature and imagine a mass of them, too weak to get off their backs, could be it."

"Something bit that messenger multiple times."

"Any man can be stupid enough to fall into a pit of vipers without the conclusion that the snakes must have gotten their legs back from God and chased after him."

"We need to prepare."

"And you'll be going on your little trip to see what's what, Ethic. Like the rest of the town agreed, I too will hear your report and consider the next steps."

"By then it will be too late."

"Nonsense. You can't know that. Even the ones that can't walk, can't run. You're not telling me you've seen running zombies, Ethic. Are you?"

"They walk relentlessly, and you heard Granby."

"I hear plenty enough from him every damn day on every subject under the sun. Just because he is old and has seen things before our time doesn't mean he knows everything or even half what he claims to be sage in."

"I'll not argue that, but I say if we're not patching the fences now, if we're not pulling in stores for a possible siege, if we're not preparing arms and evacuating the outer farms from the path, then it might well be too late by the time we return with a report."

"Farmers abandoning their lands and stabling their animals for God knows how long in this season? Madness. Giving up our livelihood on rumor."

"It was a sealed message. More than rumor. The messenger's wounds bear him witness."

"So you say, so you said, and so you were voted down."

"I can't be in both places. I can't scout there and prepare here all at once. If others don't do their share . . . "

"I'll not have you even hint that I'm not doing my share. No disrespect intended to your wet work and whatnot, Ethic, but I'll not have you stand before my calloused hands and lined face to imply my years of farming have been anything less than my share and more."

"You know I say nothing of the sort, Bay. You know I'm not insulting you as I beg you to lead the others in making preparations in my absence. Nothing in the vote prevents us from doing that, but it prevents me as I do my part in scouting north with the others."

"And nothing stops others from doing whatever they like in my stead. I made my beliefs clear on this matter before the full body."

"You know the ayes were largely not landowners. They lack the resources and leadership to head up this effort in my stead."

"That lack of landowner support should tell you something."

Ethic turned completely away and took a few steps from the ditch where the ignored zombie clawed at the air with the remainder of his fingers. I tried to follow Ethic's gaze and to divine his thoughts. He stared sort of in the direction of the high tower that was a hazy impression from this distance. He sort of faced the direction of the ruins that Ethic would only be able to survey in his mind and memory from this place. Maybe he stared somewhere between those two at nothing in particular.

"It tells me we are in trouble," he finally said.

"You best finish assembling your party and get moving."

"I have to take them into the ruins first, Bay. I can't take untested travelers into the heart of a horde without preparing them, not with what must be done."

"Wise. As you say, preparation is important but costly. Especially considering the unlikelihood of it being true."

"Would you let me take your son as part of the party?" Ethic asked.

"What say you?"

Ethic turned to stare at my father's face, both men in squint. "I said, since it is nothing to fear, and the boy is of age, let me take him as the last man of my party. It would be a good adventure for him on his path to manhood. A historic moment he will be a part of."

"Enough of that."

Ethic pressed, "No more danger than a bug on its back in a ditch, as you say, sure."

"Cease this talk."

"Let me go, Dad. I want to do it!" I was excited by the idea of leaving Dry Stretch for the first time in my life. So much so that I forgot any possibility of zombie hordes. I did not read the true dynamic of the offer between the men. "Dad?"

"No, I'll have none of it!"

Even the zombie in the ditch was startled by my father's outburst. It gave one click and squeak from its dry throat.

"And there it is," Ethic said. "The truth of your heart's heart. That is why we must prepare, for the same case against sending your son, because maybe, just maybe. If you'd not send him with me into the peril we know is out there, and I don't blame you one bit, I witness, then allow him to join you in repairing the zombie fence and storing for siege and evacuation. Please, Bay."

"You've overstayed your welcome, Ethic. Go now. Get started on preparing your party and leave us be."

My dad stabbed the sharp point of a crooked stick between the eyes of the zombie in the ditch. The tight flesh of its pale forehead split in three places and then folded in. The skull collapsed and deflated like something soft with rot. Black brains swelled and then oozed. The face was gone as the hands folded uneven over its sunken chest where clothing had dissolved into flesh. My father dropped the crooked stick into the ditch with the stilled zombie.

The stink was noxious and everywhere.

Ethic stood a moment longer. He moved his lips as if chewing or preparing to speak. He decided against it and left as he was told.

I was deeply disappointed at the offer of adventure being so quickly presented and retracted in one motion, but I knew better than to say any more. I just moved to drag the body out by its feet to the burn pile that had seen the messenger turned to ash.

My father brought up a halting hand, and I flinched. "This one will come apart and soil our hands, if we try. We'll set him ablaze in the ditch. The weeds need clearing anyway."

And that's what we did. The flames that lighted the liquifying corpse turned a different color from the natural fire spreading both directions on both sides. It was the sort of blue-green shade of burning chemicals. It burned low and long like oil touched by flame.

Had to watch that ditch a long time for the fire to finish. When I grew bored of tending it to be sure nothing spread into the rest of the field, I'd steal a glance of the hazy high tower, and I plotted against my father's wishes.

4

As Ethic sat down in the meeting of the full body following the reading of the message, yielding to Granby, my elder great-grandfather began to speak. "We have grown complacent and comfortable with the undead among us, or not among us, really, the way we live. Probably whole days go by without you thinking about them at all, the way we don't think much about wolves or gators until a pack of them drifts into our area. And why would you, if you don't remember how it used to be? I'm old enough to remember a little, not all the way back to the beginning of things, but still enough. My father died in the wars, torn apart by the feral undead. My own grandfather was surrounded, brought down, and eaten right in front of my eyes. Happened as we fled our house when a horde fell upon us, swept over our meager homestead one day. Saw him eaten. He died screaming and choking on his own blood. I ain't trying to be dramatic, but I remember what these monsters are really capable of in a large enough group. That horde the day my grandfather died was fearful stuff, but from the sounds of it, was a fraction of what overtook Brady Hollow. We need to take this message seriously. I've seen what happens when a real horde comes in when we're unprepared. I don't want to see it again."

The hall was eerily silent. No one even moved enough to make a pew pop or groan under them. Granby nodded, apparently satisfied with the sober air his words had inspired.

"I hope that was as short as I promised, Ethic. And as I promised, I yield back to you for your piece."

Granby sat and Ethic rose to a much more attentive audience than when he was first about to speak. "I think elder Granby said better than I could how serious this really is. I'll only add what I have seen in the present, as I clear the ruins and patrol the reaches around our territory. The number of zombies has increased in recent days. Some are wandering in from farther afield. Have to be or the ruins would be swept clean long ago. These are slow, as zombies are relative to humans, but they are on the move, hungry, and strong. I've not seen a proper horde as of yet, but there are clusters. A pocket of the undead will wander out together on the move or drawn by a noise. Even a few of them that are still mobile can do some damage if they get into the inner territories and catch us unaware. I do my best to weed them out, and I have. I say this to affirm that something is changing. Maybe it is truer to say that things appear to be changing back to the sort of creatures that roamed in Granby's day and before. I believe the message we heard here today. I believe the senders gave us a rare blessing of forewarning that may save us all if we but listen and prepare. We need to repair the fences, we need to arm, we need to gather supplies in case we do have to hunker down behind freshly prepared defenses, and we want to evacuate the outer farms and properties in the path of the coming horde."

That last bit brought the crowd back to life as property owners started their grumbling again.

"I've said my piece," Ethic shouted over and sat back down.

Jetty called for order. Glorigold stood and started speaking without first being acknowledged. Jetty granted her the floor a few words into her rebuttal, but by then the crowd recognized her authority and they listened.

I ditched my work and hopped the fence. I'm not sure if I knew my father was too far away to keep track of me and my doings, but I didn't care in that moment. I ran across neighbors' fields and clusters of remaining timber, making a crow's path to the tower.

The way was clear and the dust low, so the structure stood out stark, crisp, and inviting to a boy up to no good.

I just held my hand protectively over the stolen property hidden in my pouch and ran the whole way.

Arriving at the tower, I stared up through the twists and edges of its crumbling glory. Eleven floors of the structure still remained in that day, all open to the air. There were probably more than that the day it was built, judging from the spires of broken concrete sticking up from the top. I climbed the stairs until those gave out. I scaled ladders until those rose no further. Then, I went hand over hand through the bent and rusted rebar until I perched on the top flat with the wind above the tower and above its hill ripping through my hair and clothes.

I never really felt afraid until I was already at the top and could see what I'd done. I know if my dad read this, he'd say it was my worst quality.

Digging through my pouch of stolen things, I retrieved the looking glass. It was a prized thing but seldom used. Was a toss-up whether anyone would notice it missing from its shelf or not. I was certain I was going to drop it and bash the prized piece into trash upon the broken concrete debris below.

Extending the tube, I closed one eye and set the other to the lens as I lay on my belly too close to the uneven and unprotected edge. It took me a while to focus, but finally, I found the ruins and made them jump right to my face from all this great distance.

It took longer to finally locate Ethic and the ladies who followed him into the twists and turns of those dead streets. I recognized Yellow and Locust right away. It made sense that they joined him. They were two of the few who actually voted with Ethic, Granby, Aleo, and the others. There was one other woman I didn't recognize and lost her behind the crumbling walls before I could place her. There might have been others, but I didn't see them.

I grew impatient as I tried to spy them again. Fortunately for me, they stepped out into the broad highway past where a number of buildings had long ago collapsed. I could see Ethic, Locust, and Yellow again. I could only see part of a fourth. Any others were still hidden from me.

Ethic stepped out ahead of the others with his long blade up and ready. I scanned out and spotted a zombie, two zombies, maybe a half dozen, the most I had seen together in a group. Just as Ethic had said, these were up and walking, hungry and reaching.

If the horde proved to be multiples of this scene, I feared what lay ahead for Dry Stretch. I was excited too though.

As Ethic hacked away, drove the zombies back, and felled them to the ground, I was too excited to hold the looking glass straight anymore. I compressed it and ran back to climb down the perilous tower.

I had to see more, I decided.

Much could be seen from the tower in those days because of its surviving height, but it was far from everything. My chest burned, my side hitched, and my legs were full of acid, yet I ran for all I was worth, leaving the farmland behind and running through open barren lands until the first buildings of the old city ruins rose into view even with ground level. After that, it was still quite a run to get into and between the ruins themselves.

The main road and old highway through what survived of the old city was impossible to miss. It ran the whole width through the middle of all those dilapidated structures as old as the tower itself. It even stretched far enough to exit the ruins, turn north near the river, and became several miles of the riverside road itself between us and Silence Bay.

"Impossible to miss" is still a terrible direction because you can always get turned around and confused in a strange place. I entered exactly where Ethic and his party entered, I was sure. I was mostly sure, I suppose. Down on ground level, I weaved between scrap metal oxidized beyond salvage and debris fields stacked stories high between surviving buildings. Most of the time there only seemed to be one way to go. A couple times the squeeze through sharp or broken edges seemed to be tight for it to be the proper path, so I started to doubt myself. It didn't seem to take this long for Ethic and the others to emerge on their road for the training. I was afraid to turn back though.

Coming into a weedy clearing with nasty privet bushes mocking trees with their unkempt size, I climbed up onto a pile of ancient concrete slabs perched and inclined over a large metal behemoth of a wheeled vehicle large enough to be a wealthy tradesman's barge. I climbed up onto the crumbling top edge of one of those massive slabs. In the open there, I could not figure out for the life of me where these massive pieces had collapsed from. It wasn't my job to figure out the history of the rubble. I just needed the height to get some vantage on the highway.

I took out my stolen spyglass and employed it in my search. I thought I saw a piece of the highway ahead of me in the direction it should have laid, which was promising. It still seemed far, like I had doubled back on myself without realizing it. With the contours, it was still difficult to see clearly. That could have been any piece of road I was seeing the edge of out there, but I told myself it had to be the main highway. I needed it to be.

The banging and clanging rose behind me. I'd been discovered. My first wild thought was that my father had found me. My second was that Ethic had spotted me, interrupted the training, and was coming to collect me to tell my father. Those were the first two and worst things I could imagine happening to me at that age and in a world where zombies were straggling vermin to be poked with a stick and burned.

I was so startled, I kept the lens to my eye as I turned about and caught the blurry motion approaching. I adjusted the focus instead of lowering it and got a close-up view of a green face with blackened teeth. The flesh around the cheeks was split into the rotten layers of flesh. A pale and spotted tongue licked out between those teeth and its growls finally carried to my ears. The eyes weren't bright, but they were focused on me. Arms out, split fingers opening and closing, and it was walking through the weeds of privet toward me with all the energy it needed to keep shuffling along forever.

I lowered my glass, and he was much closer than I'd thought. He wasn't alone either. Two more lively zombies trailed behind him with hardly a stitch of clothing still clinging to their awful flesh. One was a woman. Her breasts sagged and rotted around the fat nipples. Her sex was a dark split wound that had to be longer and wider than it had been in life. I prayed that was not how they looked alive, or I understood why there were so few babies born in the world. The naked undead man had most of his manhood shriveled and dried small between his legs.

Three zombies! This was the most I had ever seen together up close in real life like this. And they were all walking still, toward me.

I swung off the side away from the approaching trio but found nowhere to grip. I had climbed up there, but in my panic, I'd lost the way. I tumbled over, off, and down, losing the precious spyglass as it rolled ahead of me.

Impacting the cluttered ground hard, I lost my wind and just laid there with my vision threatening to fade out on me. I watched the glass roll into the shaded crevice in the fissure between concrete plates. Even with the dead's growls surrounding me, I crawled forward, reached into that dark space, and stretched for the stolen eyeglass.

The ground shifted under me, but I ignored it. I was disoriented and afraid. Should have been afraid of being eaten alive and torn to pieces by cold, dead hands, but my fear lay in losing my father's treasure and then having to face him after I'd done so. I think fear of your father saves your life and generally turns you into a man who properly fears God and respects the danger in the world all around us. Women figure it out from watching men be idiots, Aleo tells me. In some cases, like that day trying to retrieve the spyglass instead of running for my life, fear of my father nearly saw me dead at least and probably undead to boot.

It sounded like one of them had circled around behind me, but I couldn't tell with my head turned to the side and pressed into the rough under-edge of the concrete as I stretched and reached. The naked man shuffled around into view from the other direction though. He moved slowly, but it looked much faster with him coming toward me and up on his feet like the stories of the first zombies from the Great Fall. Sweat stung my eyes, and I couldn't focus on his shape to see exactly how close he was getting.

I got my fingertips on the smooth side of the spyglass's tube and managed to roll it toward me. But then it slipped from under my sweaty fingers and rolled away again. I gave a little groan of frustration and pressed harder into that gap, harder into the rough concrete, harder into the pain.

The ground shifted again, making the world feel spongy under me, but that was the same moment the dead woman with the dark rotten nipples wandered into view behind the man. After her, a third followed. I could hear the one behind me drawing closer and the growls overlapped one another, making it clear there was more than one coming for my blindside.

So, five, at least? Maybe six? Maybe more!? My father had to hear and believe this witness now. If so many crept together in the ruins so close to our homes, there could be a horde of impossible size beyond. He had to believe the message was true after this. He might've believed it all the more if I got ravaged and turned myself.

The dirt just under the edge of the concrete lifted up in a small dome and quivered. I recognized the pattern as being that of a disturbed mole. The creature was going to be very disturbed if it drew the attention of one of these zombies. Its best move would have been to bury itself deep and hide. I sure wanted to bury myself and hide forever in that moment.

Damn it, they were getting close.

I got fingers on the curved metal again. Instead of trying to roll it into my grasp this time, I walked my fingers along its length and twisted the tapered end toward me. I heard and felt it scrape as it turned, and I showed my teeth in a new wave of fear of my father's coming wrath.

As I was still drawing the glass out carefully, I rolled over to see how close the ones behind me had gotten. I was sure they were on me. But there was no one there. Lying on my back and looking up at the sky, the echoes I had confused for another set of the undead hemming me in turned out to be phantoms in my own fearful head.

The original three I had already seen were closing in and were now close enough for me to smell the sharp stink of their death rot, but I could run in the direction of the phantoms and get away. I'd hook around the concrete slabs on that side and turn for home.

My desire to see Ethic at work up close and to experience the adventure of zombie slaying like some mythical hero of generations long past had evaporated within me. The rotten reality killed the romance of the adventure.

I had no more than rolled up into a seated position when the fourth zombie finally revealed itself. The quivering dome of the mole broke open, and the grey hand clawed out at me from the ground with dry dirt cascading off it and from between the chewed fingers.

The hand added a wrist, then a forearm, and finally bent out of the ground from a bulbous elbow joint. It curled toward me like a scorpion's stinger. Instead of striking with venom, it pawed at me and then wrapped up into a fistful of my shirt. I tried to pull away and failed. I got my first up-close experience with the undead strength of an active zombie.

The harder-packed ground shifted again. The top layer fissured and folded open in flat chunks that mimicked the great concrete slabs slanted above us. Now the head with the real threat of stinging, fatal venom rose out of the shallow grave.

The other three coming close to joining into the feast were awful things, but this soulless horror from under the earth was death itself. Eyeless sockets depressed into the face in dry, open pits. Its nose was a decayed pair of slits with a sliver of cartilage dividing them in the center. It had no tongue left but wasn't missing a single tooth, as the jaws opened wider and wider. A low rumble rose up out of its chest, through the dark throat, and out into my face on its cold breath. Through its shriveled cheeks, the cords on both sides stood out taut.

The monster held me, reached for me, teeth first, and delayed me as the others arrived.

6

As Ethic took his seat near the front of the hall and Glorigold was already speaking just a few seats over from him, I noticed how angry she looked. She had always struck me as irritable and put out any time I saw her. There was always some business going on that she found distasteful and inconvenient. Glorigold was just one of those women who looked angry in the face even when she was feeling nothing.

As the mayor granted her the floor a few words into the rant, Glorigold looked absolutely furious at the distasteful and inconvenient business she was forced to endure there that evening.

"I'm surprised I'm even having to take the time to say this. A few zombies that got their feet under them and a cryptic communication from a chewed-up messenger are hardly enough to turn our entire lives, livelihoods, and society upside down without taking the time to confirm the truth."

She paused long enough to let the crowd mumble their agreement, but not long enough for anyone to mistake it for an invitation to interrupt.

Glorigold puffed up her chest and continued. "We are seriously talking about evacuating our farms based on a rumor from hysterical men? Abandoning our land? You'll face a horde then for sure, but it'll be one of crows, rats, and coyotes; not zombies."

Laughter traveled through the hall. Didn't care for that hysterical man stereotype then or now.

"Even the idea of diverting resources toward old fences and barriers is premature. If we imagine a horde of zombies wandering in our general direction, it would still be a shuffling pace and utterly directionless. A man with his mind right could get lost trying to get here over twenty-five miles. Imagine a mindless corpse navigating that same distance. Imagine the rotting dead staying together over such a distance. Even if we could indulge such fantasy, we'd have time to survey the situation and plan. Then, once we've sent scouts to see for ourselves, we could decide the proper course of action. Maybe a few perfunctory defenses might be in order. From that distance, it would likely serve us just as well to lead them away. Instead of waiting to be sieged, we distract the stupid corpses and send them out into the barrens to wander away from us forever. When the time comes to vote, I'm pushing the commonsense approach that we send out scouts before we do anything else that might waste resources and property. That's my say."

The crowd cheered her and whistled as she took her seat again. Even that positive reaction to her words seemed to irritate her.

The cheering descended into private side discussions across all the pews. My father sat silent and waited. I wanted to talk to him about all this, but I thought it best to copy his silence.

Mr. Half stood up next, but Jetty scanned the room looking to the others, surveying the mood. Her husband raised his hand, but she still didn't acknowledge him. He started waving at her in an exaggerated way. It distracted the room enough that conversation started to waver just a little. Half was practically jumping up and down by the time Mayor Jetty rolled her eyes at his antics. A few people chuckled.

Half finally called out, "Come on, Jetty. No one is ever going to accuse you of showing me favoritism. Just give me the floor for a moment."

That brought a good bit more laughter, and she conceded him the floor.

7

I started pushing backward with my feet but only succeeded in pivoting in place at the end of that terrible arm. I also kicked loose dirt up into the unburied zombie's emaciated face. The clods landed in his open mouth and dribbled out from between his teeth, but he didn't care. The dead man from under the ground continued to excavate himself and hold onto me.

I scraped myself against the underside of the concrete in my attempt to free myself, but I was getting nowhere as I turned on the end of the strong grip. Continuing around, the fat elbow joint crunched and then snapped backward the wrong way. A thrill of hope shivered up through me but quickly extinguished as breaking his damned arm didn't prove to be enough to make him let go. Now, my twisting and shuffling only served to help draw him out of the ground further as I pulled on the end of his grip with the broken arm skewed up behind his back.

The naked man arrived first. I inhaled his fetid breath and gagged. Never smelled anything like it. Made my eyes water and nearly shut down all my senses. It's like my brain couldn't process it. I was dead to rights. I was dead before the terrible horde even arrived.

He leaned over me and pawed at me like he was petting me. The skin of his palms was as rough as bark, unforgiving against my cheeks. He was trying to find somewhere to get ahold of me, tear into me, or pull me into his teeth for a taste.

I screamed and flailed. Knocked his hands away but didn't do much to free myself.

Finally coming back to my senses too late, I started trying to shuck off my shirt to get free, but they were on me.

The naked woman behind the dead man walked into his back. Her left tit burst from the impact. Hard yellow fat bulged from the broken side of the thin skin over the breast. The skin tore along the perimeter of the black saucer of the nipple, and it flapped from side to side on a stretchy bit of flesh. A tangle of dark veins and wormy-looking flesh showed through the round opening.

I gagged again.

The pawing man was bent over at the waist, and the woman knocked him over. Stumbling over the undead thing crawling out of the ground, more joints cracked and broke. The zombie rolled free of the dirt as it still tried to hold on.

Fingers snapped off of the hand like the sound of breaking carrots. I rolled over backward twice before I got my head back out of the neck of my rumpled shirt.

I didn't like what I saw. As I forced myself up to my feet to run, I had two of them on one side and two on the other. They were all coming for me.

Nearly tripped over my own feet twice trying to get away, but I managed to stay upright and really started to move in the only direction I could go—deeper into the city.

I had seen the passthrough from up on those slabs, but running wild through the field with no less than four zombies on my trail, I couldn't have found a wide open arch with a welcome sign. There was a stretch of tilted cinderblock wall too high for me to reach the top and still too steep to climb. I ran first one way and then another, finding nothing but twisted and rusted chain-link and scrap metal from ages past. No route of escape. No possibility of egress. And those four monsters were getting closer in their steady, unhurried, unrelenting fashion.

I found a narrow gap in the fencing. It was not the gap I had spied earlier, and it wasn't wide. I squeezed through anyway, succeeding in tearing my clothes and scratching my arms on the sharp ends on both sides.

I hissed through the pain of it and retreated away. I knew I needed to find a way around and back out of the city. The first undead man slipped through, tearing the skin down to his dark ribs on one side. He didn't pause or wince in the least, his uneven dead eyes fixed upon me.

The naked female corpse followed, shredding one of her breasts on the way through. With no concern for the state of her body, she shoved at the fellow in front of her to try to get to me first.

Turning to run yet deeper into the ruins, I fled before the last two found their way through the gap as well. I weaved down the slopes and across the crumbling foundations of missing structures. I crossed what could have been roadways, but they were buried in dirt and overgrown with all manner of worthless plants. What I was not finding was the main highway that might lead me out of here toward the river or give me more ground to leave the zombies behind.

I realized that I was making a noise. It took me a while to identify it as my voice because it sounded so unlike me, barely human at all. It was high, shrill, and choppy, a sound of unhinged terror. I wasn't calling for help. I was leaking my pure fear that had grown too big and awful inside me to contain any longer. It served as a siren to help the undead to track me easily through the city.

One false step as I pushed through a patch of tall grass, and I fell. My foot swung through empty air where I expected more ground to be. It was a wonder I didn't impale or split myself open on all the rebar on the broken concrete wall as I tumbled down the incline into a recess of roadway.

The undead followed me over. They tumbled, snapped bones, left a skinning of rotten flesh behind, and rose faster than me to continue the pursuit. As I staggered out across the deeply faded blacktop, I barely limped ahead of them with all four right on me. I squeaked and whined out my fear again.

Then I was grabbed, as I knew I would be. Like countless other stupid boys before me through the ages, I was going to be brought down and eaten alive, screaming with no one to hear me or save me. I was going to die painfully as my foolishness deserved.

Ethic Hanover held on even as I struggled to get away. He quickly wheeled me around behind him and shoved me straight down to the cracked surface of the highway. I sat down hard with a bone-jarring landing that clacked my teeth together.

He raised his weapons on the four monsters staggering toward us, the ones I had drawn out.

Locust swung a blade on the end of a stick that looked a lot like a shovel. It split open a skull on one side and then she swung across the other way, decapitating the body next to the first. The headless form folded straight down and belched out black blood and gore. The head twirled and then bounced away up one of the lanes.

I tried to calm my breathing. Two were gone already. But no. There were still four left, the same four that had been following me. How?

The two Locust had killed with her sharp shovel were extra. They had already been here, part of the team's training. My God, there had been six of them in one place now. How could anyone doubt the message and the threat that faced us now?

Yellow moved up beside Ethic on one side with hammers in her hands. Liberty stood on the other holding a curved blade a bit larger than a standard machete. Liberty was the extra person I hadn't identified from my earlier spying. That was odd because she had voted against the measures put forward before the full body. What was she doing here then?

Saving my foolish hide at the moment was what she was doing.

Locust jogged up quickly to join the others.

I looked around myself where I sat useless on the ground. I expected to see more of the lively undead crawling out of every shadow and out from under every piece of debris. The world had shifted on its axis for me. It was suddenly full of undead threat. They could be anywhere. They were everywhere. This persistent global terror I felt had to be what the people felt at the beginning of it all, when the world went from peaceful to overwhelmed by reanimated corpses. I was foolish. We were all foolish for downgrading the threat in our minds to a minor nuisance. There were monsters at our doorsteps, probably, even more, stalking down upon us, and we were ignoring it at our own peril.

Ethic attacked with two long blades at once. He stabbed the dead woman, who had shredded boobs, and drove the blade through her eye and out the back of her head. The other blade went up through an undead man's nose and out the top of his mangy crusted scalp, turning the top of his head into a bloom of pink, curdled cottage cheese, and purple-grey spongy matter.

I vomited up my breakfast into a modest puddle on the highway between my thighs. I saw a swirl of colors and textures that reminded me of the brain flower sprouting from the dead man's head. I threw up some more in a far less modest puddle that splattered my clothes this time.

As I looked away from my mess, so I wouldn't have to think about it anymore, I saw the two pursuers Ethic had addressed now felled in the lane at his feet.

Yellow used her hammers to pummel the forehead of a third zombie from the cluster that had followed me. It kept reaching out like it wanted to hug her as she kept knocking its head first one way and then the other. She was reshaping his face but not bringing him down. I thought that would continue forever as he would eventually wrap her up and bring her down to feed.

I also thought Ethic was just going to stand there and let it happen. But then its head caved in with abrupt force. Chunks of brain dribbled out and down the remains of his face from several openings. He bowed forward and went limp everywhere down his body except for his stiff legs with his knees locked out. Yellow stepped back and to the side, allowing the dispatched zombie to faceplant across where she had been standing, like a man knocked out from a bar fight.

Ethic spoke clearly and calmly as he said, "You have to do that quicker. Every shot has to count in moments like this."

As he was instructing in a manner that befit a schoolhouse better than a zombie-infested highway, Liberty swung her curved blade through the last zombie left in the immediate area. This was the dry, sandy one that had pulled free of the ground to attack me. He was taller than the rest now that he was fully standing out there in the open. She drew back so far that she nearly caught Ethic's shoulder with her backswing. I'm not sure he even saw it as he was addressing Yellow's work.

Liberty's first cut caught more throat than head. The loose skin there collapsed to reveal the flexing cords within the throat and a goodly portion of the jawbone on that side. She stepped back and he pressed forward. She swung again in a wild arc from left to right.

This time, Yellow took Ethic by the shoulder and pulled him out of range of Liberty's blade. It was a close call. He might have dodged it himself being who he was, but no telling for sure.

She carved through the dry skin of the zombie's forehead and dented the skull underneath deep, but she didn't break into the brain, and the monster didn't go down. More than the sharpness of the cut, the blunt force of the attack set the undead man from his shallow grave staggering back. His poor coordination tripped him up and sent him stumbling to the side, but he didn't fall down yet. It did give a little breathing room though.

"Watch it!" Ethic ordered.

Liberty glanced back at him before turning her attention on the zombie again. "I am watching. I got him."

"Not him," Ethic said. "The rest of us. If you cut one of us with a wild swing, you'll infect us. It'll be as fatal as a bite."

"I'm watching."

"You are not. You nearly cut me just now, and you didn't realize it."

"Can we talk about this after this thing is dead, please?"

Locust swung three times with her shovel thing from behind the sandy creature. The first strike opened up its shoulder above the bent and twisted arm he had grabbed me with earlier. The damaged cartilage showed there. I'm not sure what she hit exactly on the next swing, but a couple flaps of dry skin sheered away and flew out onto the roadway beside him. They had crisp, natty hair on one side. Her third attempt broke through the back of its head, and he fell backward, landing with a thump. His knees were bent up and out at odd angles. That was finally the end of him.

"Any encounter that ends with us alive and uninfected is a good one," Ethic said, "but we have to be more efficient and effective with our strikes or we risk not coming out alive in encounters that might be more harried than this one."

Locust nodded and turned away as she stalked up the road at an angle.

"Liberty," Ethic said.

She turned around.

"Be aware of your surroundings so you don't end up hurting one of us."

"I could have killed that one. She didn't have to do it for me."

"I know you could, but I need you to acknowledge what I said."

"Do you want me to just leave Ethic? Would that be easier?"

He tilted his head. "I need you to be willing to take instruction, Liberty. Does that work for you, I hope?"

"I can take instruction."

"Then, more efficient strikes and be aware of where we all are so we can protect each other and come out of this alive."

"Fine."

"Hopefully, we can see what needs to be seen and come back without getting into any trouble. Maybe get back in plenty of time to warn the others." He turned to face me.

"Don't tell my father," I blurted out. I turned to the side to spit out the sour taste in my mouth.

Turning that way, I saw Locust move a piece of rust-eaten metal aside to reveal a severed head. Its eyes rolled in their sockets and its teeth clicked together loud enough to hear from where I was sitting. Locust flipped her shovel over and used the metal-tipped point to drive down into the temple of the undead head. It penetrated with a soft squish, and the animated head relaxed.

Efficient.

I managed not to vomit again, which I considered quite a victory in that moment. I backed away from the mess I made before standing. I shifted to the side as dizziness spotted my vision. Yellow moved fast enough to steady me by my shoulder. Then, she pulled her hand away from me and wiped it off on her trousers.

She was always rather nice to me, I recall.

"Don't tell your father?" Ethic asked.

"Yes, please, sir. I'm sorry I intruded."

"I'm sorry you did too," Ethic said. "Do you have any idea how thin my relationship is with your father right now? With the entirety of Dry Stretch, but especially your father?"

"Because of me," I said. I couldn't look him in the eye.

As Locust returned to the group, Liberty said, "Probably because of all the shouting the other night more than the kid, right?"

Yellow asked me, "Are you bitten, boy?"

"I'm not," I mumbled. "I scratched myself on some concrete and fencing. Nothing more. I'm not bitten or even scratched by . . . them."

Ethic cut his eyes at Liberty. She furrowed her brow and shrugged. "I'm just saying. Maybe your troubles with Master Bay are about the kid, but probably not the thinness with the whole town."

"Fair enough." He attended back to me. "Unfortunately for you, I can't keep this from your father. It will be a hard enough thing when he is told. Will probably still blame me for it in part even if you tell the truth that I had nothing to do with you being here. Will be worse if I try to cover for you. What we are doing is far too important and fragile at the moment. Lives are at stake, not even broaching how foolishly you risked yourself for no good reason. I know wrath awaits you, but no amount of grace is going to change that now. Like all the dark business we are here to address, it's a hard truth that must be faced."

I protested further. It was weak rebellion at best, but I tried. At some point along the way, I gave up as they marched me out of the ruins and back for home to face my father. Ethic's path was easier walking, but I'd have been happier to be assailed by a cluster of zombies twice over than facing my father, if given the choice.

Ethic took me back to my father, and there was wrath indeed.

8

After Half, husband of the mayor, made the room laugh, Jetty conceded him the floor before the full body, and he took it.

"I know there is a lot of tension and that has the potential for hard feelings, but we are a community and can work together to figure out what is going on here. I remember during the droughts as the tough job of farming and ranching became even tougher, we—"

"Get to your point, Half," Jetty ordered from the podium.

He cut her a look, but I noticed he broke eye contact first.

"Right, well, my point is that there are good points on both sides. The point of agreement, however, seems to be in sending out a scouting party. We should probably vote on that, and then we can decide as a majority whether we agree to start more formal defensive preparations here as some have suggested. Obviously, Ethic should lead the scouting party, I think, and we'll need some volunteers for that. Whatever they report back, we can use that information to make our next decision, no matter how the second vote on preemptive preparations goes. Does anyone care to volunteer for a little jaunt with Ethic to see what might be happening in the north of—"

Jetty cut him off again. "You don't take volunteers for an expedition before the expedition is voted on."

"We don't need anyone's permission to leave town," someone shouted from the back. "Whoever wants to go look, just go."

"And whoever wants to defend their property can prepare to do so. I don't even know why we're here."

Half waited for order to restore or for Jetty to demand it of the full body, but side discussions and shouting escalated instead.

Ethic stood up and Half cut him a look. It seemed to me to be sort of a mix between gratitude that Ethic might be restoring order on Half's behalf and mild irritation that Ethic was taking the floor without asking Half to yield it. Everyone was going to forget Half had it in the first place, if they hadn't already.

"Enough of this," Ethic shouted. "We are on the verge of losing our town and the argument is over votes and the nature of reality itself. It doesn't matter what any of us wishes was true. What you guess is happening doesn't change what is. With respect to each of you and all your various positions in our body, open your heads. Everyone with experience fighting these things and dealing with them past or present is telling you we are in trouble, so we are in trouble. That messenger was bitten. He didn't just lay there and let one sluggish zombie in a ditch chew on him for the fun of it."

The crowd didn't quiet all the way down. A few laughed at Ethic's quip, and most were attending to him despite the din of noise.

He continued, "He fought his way through multiple undead monsters. He was bitten several times for his effort. He kept coming south anyway despite the fever and the bone aches and the delirium that was setting over him."

"If he was delirious," Glorigold stood slowly, but spoke loudly, "then nothing he said can be trusted."

"Nice try," Ethic shouted as the crowd chatter increased again, "but a message from the mayor of the town sealed in wax is not a delirious statement. It is a witness to the truth."

"We don't know what is really out there," Glorigold said, "until trustworthy people go out and survey it for us. It is foolish to take action before that."

"We do know what is out there," Ethic said back. "We know exactly. We've been told by authority, and we saw the results on the messenger who sacrificed himself to warn us. It is a dishonor to him and to ourselves to pretend otherwise."

"I will not have anyone dictate to me how I handle my business or my life," Glorigold yelled. Her workers had heard it often from her and were used to it, even though it never stopped scaring them. Most of the full body was shocked to silence by how harsh and crackingly loud her voice had gotten in her argument across the room with Ethic. "I'm not turning my world upside down on what is yet unsubstantiated, and I'll not have a breeder and cadaver dog lecture me on any subject."

A gasp passed through the room.

I whispered to my father, "What does that—"

"Quiet, boy. Stay out of it."

Ethic paused but then responded in a quiet voice that was well-heard in the shocked silence. "Your anger and insult are probably tolerated on your property because no one challenges you. Here where your opinion is no more than one vote like everyone else's, you have turned unbecoming to make up for it. We are fools if we ignore every parable ever taught us on preparation for coming ill weather for the exact reason that every foolish creature in those tales dies for shirking responsibility because of inconvenience. If we do now, then we deserve to die. As for your anger and insult, your ill behavior does not impress me."

"Nothing about you impresses me!" Glorigold bellowed red in the face.

Jetty hammered her gavel for order even though every person in the building sat frozen still with their jaws hanging agape.

9

The rest of Ethic's training party, which would be his scouting party in a few days at most, waited out by the road beyond the edge of my father's property. They wanted nothing of my father's wrath either. Ethic marched up the dirt path at my flank toward the homestead buildings.

My father stepped out on the porch and watched us approach. He said something we were too far to hear, and everyone moved inside in a hurry, everyone except Granby who remained on the creaking porch swing through the whole episode.

My father stalked down the steps and out across the dooryard. He met the head of the trail and started down to meet us partway home. I wanted to slow down to the point of moving backward to avoid my fate, but Ethic gave me a soft but firm hand to my back to let me know there was no stopping or retreating to be had.

We met closer to the home than the road.

"What is this?" my father asked in an even tone that was thick with threat.

Ethic said, "I was in the ruins with the party, preparing for our scouting expedition, when he came crashing unto the scene with the hungry dead in tow. We were able to put them down and save his skin to bring him home to you whole."

"Is that so?"

"I offer you my witness to it."

"Your influence on the boy of late, his draw to you, and your business is disheartening."

Ethic shifted on his heels beside me. "My business is requiring all my attention. He's lucky to have survived his little adventure."

"I'll be happy when you and yours are on your way and this is behind us. He can better focus on his work."

"I'll tell you, Bay, I don't like your implication that him showing up was any of my doing."

"Was it not at all, Ethic?"

"Each man is responsible for his own choices and the consequences therein."

"I agree with you completely, and so here we are again."

Ethic shifted again and I thought he was going to leave. Much of me wishes he had.

But he said, "I'm tasked with the zombies, the training of a party, and an expedition into dangerous territory we have already been warned about by a dead messenger. That has my full attention. I would appreciate it if you would keep an eye on your own boy, so I'm not saving him and bringing him back to you prodigal."

"You'll watch your tone with me, Ethic Hanover. You'll watch it close."

"I'll watch it as closely as you watch your implications of any of this being my fault, Bay. I'll watch it closer than you watch him."

"You test me, Ethic. You test the bounds of our friendship such as it is."

"I'm not sure I can tell much difference between being your friend and being anything else. At any rate, I return your son to your charge as he ever was."

"You're leaving soon then, I hope. I look forward to wishing you well with safe travels, sir."

Ethic paused again. "He has something to return to you as well."

My father glanced at me and then back to Ethic. "How's that?"

"Show him what you took with you on your misadventure, boy."

I could have died. My hands shook and my legs grew ever weaker as I withdrew the spyglass from my bag. I heard my father's breathing change, and I waited to be struck down. Instead, he lifted the artifact from my grasp and turned it over several times. It was scratched along one curve of the metal nearest the forward lens. The metal looked clawed through multiple layers where I had dropped it and retrieved it in those broken concrete slabs. I might have been better off if I left it so Ethic wouldn't know I had taken it.

My father's voice shook. "This has been in my family . . . for generations. It was from the world before the first uprising."

We said nothing. My father extended and contracted the spyglass a few times. The porch swing creaked under Granby, but I didn't dare look.

"This is a great violation," my father added.

"I'll leave you to it, sir." Ethic turned away.

My father growled at his back. "You see no part in this, Ethic? None?"

"None, sir?" He had his back to my father. "If he is new to disobeying you, it is none of my mine and all of yours."

"The day you visited me after the vote to try to sway me again," my father said in a drawn, tight voice, "you thought it clever to suggest my son join you. You suggested it in his presence as a test of me to force me to admit the danger I did not want him involved in. You thought it was clever, but you did not think of the consequence of putting such an idea in a boy's head, a boy hungry for adventure but too young and dumb to understand the real danger. I said no for his sake and yours. He is responsible for his thievery and disobedience. I am responsible to discipline him for it and for keeping him out of your hair, too. But do you not see any part in your clever little quips meant to hurt me for voting against you?"

Ethic tarried only a moment longer before he resumed his retreat. "I leave you to it. Any further misadventure on his part is firmly your responsibility going forward, I think we can agree, sir."

My father stared down at his scratched spyglass as I stood and shook.

Finally, in a voice so low that it hurt my soul, he asked, "Are you bitten?"

"No, sir."

"You're sure?"

"I'm certain."

"They got no hands or teeth on you?"

"No, sir. One of them had me by the clothes for a moment, but I pulled free. Ethic and his party rescued me, as he said."

"Were you scratched during your escape or otherwise?"

"No, sir."

"I see scratches upon you."

"Yes, sir. I rolled and slid down concrete and asphalt. Nothing more. I give my witness, sir."

"The witness of a liar and thief. Come with me, boy."

He turned his back on me, still holding the spyglass, still rubbing his thumb over the scratches, and I followed him through our property, prepared for the beating of my life, if not to end it.

My father barked at the porch. "And don't think I don't know your voice chirping in his ear."

I glanced at Granby. Even he was staring hard upon me. I had no one in the world on my side in that moment. Maybe I deserved no one for what I'd done and how I acted.

We bypassed the main barn, and he took me to the toolshed off to the side. When I needed a beating, my father tended to get it over with, out in the open. Everyone knew what the phrase "taken to the toolshed" meant. I expected to be straight murdered in there.

My father opened the door with a rattle and ordered, "Step inside."

"Please, Father."

"I'll hear none of it." He still didn't raise his voice. That somehow made this all so much more terrible. "I'll have none of it. Do what I say for once today."

I stepped inside the darkness and kept my back to him as I prepared for death to come.

"Turn and face me, boy, even if you have not the honor to look me in the eyes."

I turned about in the middle of that dirt floor with walls lined by sharp metal things all around me. I kept my eyes on the sour dirt at my feet just as he predicted I would.

Running off, embarrassing him in front of Ethic and all of Dry Stretch by proxy, stealing and damaging the spyglass—there was no end to the sins he had to scold me and punish me for. No surprises here. I needed to endure whatever was to come, all of which I'd brought upon myself, down on my own head.

"We cannot risk the family."

I thought I'd misunderstood what he'd said, "What? What, sir?"

"Open your head and understand, boy."

"Yes, sir."

"Might your scratches be as you describe them, and I pray so. Might they also be something that will infect. So, you will wait out the proper number of days here. Select a bucket from the back for your wastes. We'll slide your meals under the wall and retrieve the same. Once your time passes without infection, we'll deal with all else. The solitude of quarantine may serve enough for you to think on what you did and all that's needed."

"What? I don't understand."

"You will soon enough, boy."

He swung the door closed and latched me into the dark. I flung myself forward in a panic. The door bucked in its frame from my impact, but my father was braced for it and held me in.

"No. No. No. Don't leave me in here. Don't lock me in the dark."

"Your eyes will adjust, boy. You made this necessary."

"I'm not bit. I'm not scratched. I'm not infected."

"I'll not have you put your mother or brothers at risk. This is the cost of your choices, son."

I heard the lock latch. I hadn't even seen him retrieve one.

"No! Let me out. Don't do this. Father, please, I'm sorry. Just beat me. Don't leave me in here. Please. I'm begging."

"Well, stop begging because it changes nothing except my opinion of you." My father's voice was getting farther away. "You'll be wiser for it in the end. You'll learn to accept what can't be changed."

I continued to beg after my father was well out of earshot. I expected my mother, my brothers, or Granby to come to me. I expected something from one of them. But none of them did. I was left alone except when someone slid my food under the wall or retrieved the same. I think it was my brothers, but they wouldn't speak to me. I don't know if it was my whole family ashamed of me or if they followed the angry orders of my father in fear. Either way, I felt abandoned by everyone.

I'm not sure what my father expected my takeaway to be, but I hardened in my resolve and in my rebellion as a result. I think I might have hated him then, at least for a time, but it's hard to remember clearly with everything that came next.

I did use one of the buckets, but only to hold and move dirt. I used a few of the tools as my eyes adjusted enough to distinguish them in the low light as my father said they would. It took me less than a day and two meals to dig myself out from under the secluded back corner of the shed.

I gathered what I needed from the house and stole a few things out of spite as my family slept. Then, I was away for my greatest misadventure of all.

10

"Nothing about you impresses me!" Glorigold bellowed, red in the face at poor Ethic.

Jetty hammered her gavel for order even though every person in the building sat frozen still with their jaws hanging agape.

In that shocked pause, my father stood. It seemed at first everyone was too flustered to notice, including Jetty at the reins of this contentious meeting.

People started to look back and forth at my father who stood silent and patient. He might have waited there forever.

"You wish to speak on this matter now, Bay?" Jetty asked.

"I do."

"I grant you the floor for your say, Bay."

My father took a beat and then started. "I hold great respect for both Ethic Hanover and Glorigold. They've earned as much in my estimation, and I can't imagine anyone else would have cause to disagree, no matter how heated this discussion has become."

Everyone mumbled their assent. I got the feeling that they would have agreed to most anything in that moment to relieve the tension. Angry landowners scared them more than any threat of zombie hordes. At least back then they did. All of it sort of hung on what my father decided to say next.

He continued.

11

I could hear them before I could see them. And I could smell them on the cursed winds before all that.

I was far from home and had been tracking behind Ethic's scouting party for a few days. I was not prepared. I didn't bring enough food or water. I brought more clothes than I needed though, and my pack was heavy. I knew how to take care of myself. I could hunt and trap. I could boil water to make it safe. But I had stuck to foraging mostly.

We were not close to anything I could recognize from the maps I'd seen. The main road to the other towns was farther west toward the river. They had swung way east inland. I had seen no sign of Silence Bay, Portmire, or Brady Hollow as I had expected. I had no idea how far we had traveled either.

When I topped the hill, all the false courage and bravado I had mustered to take this misadventure drained right out of me. If I didn't drop to my belly on my own, I would have collapsed out of shock and terror. I could not let them see me. They might have already smelled me as I had done them. I hoped the putrid wind was to my face.

They stretched out as far as I could see from this low rise in the trail. It was no cover at all, but they filled the land for miles in every direction leading away from me. They weren't completely shoulder to shoulder, but they were packed together. There would be no slipping through unharmed.

Not only had I never seen this many zombies at once before, but I had never seen this many of anything in one place ever. The full body gathered in the town hall of Dry Stretch was obviously the most living people I'd ever seen, but these zombies spreading out across the world outnumbered the entire population of Dry Stretch and all the surrounding farms several times over. It wouldn't occur to me until later that some of these vast numbers probably included the former living populations of the towns north of us and might include my people and family soon. The most livestock I'd seen were Glorigold's cattle and sheep grazing the hillsides along our side of the river on her vast property. This was well more than that, and if she saw this, all her protest about not jumping to conclusions would evaporate right out of her. I almost wished she was here to see this. The closest I had ever seen of a gathering this large were the flocks of birds that traveled up and down the river at certain times of the year back then. We had to cover crops and make noise to convince them to feed on the other side from our farms. Truth be told, I thought there were more zombies before me than every bird I might have seen my entire life.

The sound was loud, droning, deafening. It was more than I could process as I lay on my belly wishing to be invisible, desiring to be anywhere but right in their path. I had not seen an ocean up to that point in my life, but the day I finally did with the waves crashing on the rocks, I was brought back to this moment in my mind and had to get off my feet then too. The tide of their ruined voices washed through the air first one way and then the other.

There were buildings down there in the midst of all this rotting flesh. The dead wandered in and out of broken doorways. They circled the structures and reached through broken windows as others shuffled past without even turning their heads to look.

I retrieved the scratched spyglass I had stolen from my father a second time. I didn't even care to think how angry he was with me at that moment. I might have been safer just joining the zombies.

I focused across the tops of their awful heads at the action around the buildings. If they weren't ruins before the dead arrived, they certainly were now. None of them seemed to be feeding. I'd never seen a zombie eat a victim up to that point in my life. I'd heard it in stories and histories same as everyone else, and I wondered how zombies could eat people and make more zombies at the same time. I still had no answer. They were interested in these buildings, some of them, maybe searching for living flesh, but there didn't appear to be any to find, not anymore. At least until they found me not far down the trail.

One zombie trying to press his way through a window with shards of glass still hanging along the edges cut himself badly. I showed my teeth and nearly hissed at the magnified sight of it but forced myself to stay quiet. The discolored skin along one arm split and folded away, but the dead man kept pressing, extending the cut up his arm, past the elbow, into the underside of the purple bicep. The glass sunk in deeper and divided the muscle too.

I pulled my watering eye away from the spyglass, realizing I was on the verge of gagging and maybe coughing up my latest trail meal. I breathed through it. Had to breathe through my mouth because the humid air was noxious.

Motion caught my attention off to the northeast and deep into the horde. I was having trouble understanding this was what a horde was, more than an army, more than a herd or flock of any living thing. I had pictured a mob but one you could see all sides of at once. Even if I was on the top level of the tower, I couldn't have seen back to where their numbers ended. I had no proof they didn't extend on forever beyond the very edge of the world, bleeding out beyond our own reality.

That motion. It came with a growl that was deeper and carried further than the rest of the voices competing against each other. Even a few of the creatures nearest me turned their heads and hesitated their forward progress because of it. The energy of that motion carried through the crowd in waves. The whole horde shifted to the west and then back east again, but not quite as far as their original trajectory. They very much reminded me of birds in that moment, but I thought I understood birds to be led by the front. This steering seemed to be occurring by the back. Yet another backward thing going on here.

I brought my spyglass back up and focused as far out as I could to what I saw as the source of the waves of commotion. I didn't see it at first, and then it passed through my line of sight. I had to shift and refocus.

It was a vehicle deep within the horde. The motor grumble coming to my ears from that direction above the zombie growls and moans reminded me of some of the processing machines the more wealthy farmers manned. I'd heard about, but had never seen, one used to move a thing on wheels.

The zombies around it sort of alternated between trying to claw at the thing and whoever might be inside and losing interest before turning away to follow the others. It roared forward a few more feet as it hooked around in a wide curve through the crowd. Another wave of motion shifted through the crowd spreading out from the vehicle. A little more west, a little more toward the river.

A second motor sound carried to me, and I shifted my view westward. I saw another vehicle. This one had a taller profile but was farther away, harder to see even with the spyglass. I estimated it to be hooking in roughly the same direction as the other motorized thing.

Were these the people who went with the ruined buildings? Was this their slow escape? Maybe they desired to ease away so as not to have the zombies pin them in and trap them forever.

Dry Stretch had no such machines, and they were doing nothing to build the fences or to prepare. My family's farm was perched about as far north as you could go in Dry Stretch. Our land, our lives, would be first.

I lowered my glass and then heard growls coming from behind me. I gasped and rolled to my back, kicking up some dust as I prepared to fight and flee. None were upon me, but some of the forward undead within the horde had passed my position through the brush off the trail and to the west. A growing number of them were beyond me and behind me.

I knew they had been slowly approaching me, but I had been lulled by the slow sway of their progress. I'd fascinated myself with details in their midst. As a result, I'd been flanked and risked getting surrounded before I could retreat.

My prospects for retreat weren't great. I could run, but not forever. I could keep moving south to stay ahead of them, but I had to rest, and I'd just be leading them home with me, even if I could keep moving. I needed to try to get out and around them, but I would have to go far to the side, maybe further than I could really get as close as I'd stumbled upon them. Even if I did that, I'd be cut off, with the horde between me and home.

And home? Dry Stretch might be as doomed as every town these zombies had overwhelmed to feed their bellies and increase their numbers.

I closed up the spyglass and stowed it away. I gathered my pack and crawled backward down the low rise, hoping not to be seen before I stood to run again.

I was grabbed, jerked up from the ground, and hauled up onto my feet. I sucked in air to scream, but Ethic Hanover clapped his hand over my mouth to silence me before I could.

"Foolish boy, stay with me and run, or your life will soon be over. Don't make a sound. Move!"

I did as Ethic commanded me.

12

Everyone mumbled their assent to my father's magnanimous words, and then he continued, "We'll do what needs to be done as soon as we know what needs to be done, same as we always do with every challenge we face. The fact is that we don't truly know until we see for ourselves. If it is a fight we have, then we'll fight. If it is defense and evacuation that is called for, we'll deal with that. If this turns out to be something more or less than we think now, well, we'll make an informed decision once the time comes. We have to be informed though. There's no way around that need. I think we can talk about this all night, but ultimately, we need to vote. As has been stated by others, it's really two votes. We vote on sending a scouting party to report back. We have a vote on whether to wait on that intelligence or to act in advance of it. Like many here, I think sending the scouting party is likely to be near unanimous and those who choose to go will have my sincere thanks and respect for it. On the acting in advance vote, I think we will be more split, but we will abide by what is decided whether we like it or not. That is the purpose of the full body. I myself will be joining others to vote against acting before we know, but whatever is decided, I will abide."

The crowd applauded as my father sat.

Granby stood again, and Jetty recognized him. "My grandson-in-law lays out the decisions before us pretty succinctly. No argument there. I would hope there would be no strong objection to sending the scouting party. I differ from my kin on the attitude toward preparation. With respect, the wait-and-see approach can cost us greatly. We don't wait to see how bad the winter is going to get before we decide how much to store. When a storm comes, we watch the signs and act accordingly, but we do not wait to see how bad it really gets before we start bringing the animals in. We begin to prepare at the first signs, so we're not caught flatfooted. I know many of you would say, well, winter comes every year, and we do see the signs of a bad storm before we act, not overreacting to every drizzle. I would say we have seen what the bad seasons and undead storms of the zombies can do in numbers like the ones described in the message. It's just been so long since the winter of zombies that we've been allowed to forget and to pretend that 'never again' is ever an option in this world. Well, the storm is coming, winter is returning, and we can either prepare wisely or be caught suffering for it. So, I'm going to be voting aye and aye for the good of Dry Stretch and every soul in it."

Granby sat and Ethic stood. I heard Glorigold sigh audibly. So did many others as they turned their heads to the sound. Ethic simply waited and was recognized again.

"There's not much more or new to say, so I'll keep my last piece brief," Ethic said. "There is no margin for error with zombies. Most of us have not seen them in any real numbers in our lifetimes. They move slow if they move at all. Even in large numbers, they would move slow. That can lull us into a false sense of security. While they move slowly, they can move without stopping. In a horde, they are liable never to stop. In our confidence in that slowness, we might believe we have more time than we do. The worst floods can move slowly, but there is no standing against those natural forces in the end, not without advanced preparation. This is our window to prepare. When we have gone to see for ourselves and returned, time will be short. The steady progress of this unnatural threat can wipe us from the Earth. That's my piece. You either hear me or you don't. I will be voting aye and aye, as well."

Before Ethic was even seated, Glorigold called out, "We've heard and heard again. It's time to call for a vote on both points. Let's be done with it. Decide it and abide."

She was not recognized formally, but she was heard. The proper order of calls and seconds were made.

Neither vote was very close in the end. Ethic was charged with gathering and training volunteers for a scouting party unanimously. Everybody loves a plan that requires nothing of them. The mood to wait for the scouting party's report before making preparations had settled through over two-thirds of the room and the second vote reflected that.

Just as would have happened whether there had been a vote or not, some prepared on their own while most did nothing about it, hoping the problem would solve itself.

Granby split our house's vote, and my father didn't like it.

13

"I don't understand," I said as I crouched under a stone and metal arch half buried in years of hard runoff.

Ethic, Yellow, Locust, and Liberty gathered around me with their melee weapons at their sides. Outside and above us, the endless footsteps shuffled along. Dry loose dirt spilled off the precipice above and drifted away on the breeze. The rolling growls and moans continued like a rising storm. We were literally under them as the edge of their mindless army walked over our hiding spot.

"They won't be moved," Yellow whispered. Her voice still echoed in the tight place. "We've tried."

"I couldn't get them to stop moving after me in the ruins," I said.

Ethic gave a downward motion with his hand to indicate I needed to speak more quietly.

Locust said, "We've tried, but as soon as we shift the crowd one way to get them off course from Dry Stretch, they drift back the other, closing in on the river and home again."

One of the dead monsters above stepped too close to the edge. A wash of dirt poured down first and then the body of a dead, dry-rotted man tumbled after. Most of his limbs snapped on the way down, and his back broke at the bottom.

I held my breath for the others to come cascading down until they blocked out the sun and smothered us in our hiding spot. They kept stalking by without paying their fallen man any attention.

The zombie actually blinked a couple times like he was surprised by the fall. I don't think zombies can blink, but I swear he did.

The way his neck was twisted around, he spied us in the shadows. He started moaning again and struggled to get flipped over so he could crawl toward us, but he couldn't quite manage it. Liberty stabbed out with the sharp point of her long weapon. He relaxed and breathed out his last as his head leaked dark from his scalp.

The stench wafted into the space with us, and I waved my hand in front of my face, but it did no good.

Yellow offered me a canister of a glistening paste. I just stared at her not understanding. She wiped the pad of her thumb through it and then rubbed the stuff above my lip directly under my nostrils. I shivered from her touch. It had a burning medicinal smell that made my eyes water a little. It helped the stench a lot.

I hoped her hands were clean.

"Do you think it has something to do with those motors?" I asked.

That got everyone's attention.

Ethic finally spoke. "What motors?"

Another zombie tumbled end over end down the rough slope. She slammed face down on the ground. The female corpse bit through her pale tongue, and it fell out loose in the sand. A spill of dirt followed down on top of her, changing the color of her remaining dark hair and burying the severed tongue.

As she rose up, one of her sagging breasts had split open four ways, like meaty petals of a wilting flower. A big plastic bag rolled out from inside. There was some sort of liquid or gel inside that. It was spotted through the middle with dark black mold. I had no idea what I was seeing. For the longest time after that, I thought all women grew those moldy bags inside them, and that gel was what fed the babies. That's not how it works, but I still don't know what the hell that growth was that broke out of that dead woman that day.

Liberty kicked the woman hard in the face twice to keep her from crawling in with us. It changed the shape of the dead woman's shriveling features. Finally, Liberty stabbed down between her own feet and stilled the second body.

Ethic snapped his fingers lightly close to my ear. "Focus. What motors are you talking about?"

"There were people in the middle of the horde. Didn't see them, but they were moving in . . . I don't know. Like closed carriages with motors making them go."

Locust shook her head. "Like the ones in the ruins? Those ancient things?"

"I don't know," I said. "I just saw them and heard them. They were made of metal and had motors. Do you think those could be . . . ? I don't know what I'm trying to say."

"Motorized vehicles?" Ethic's eyes lost focus.

Yellow said, "I don't understand how that would be useful."

Three more bodies tumbled off the edge in rapid succession, crashing to the ground outside our alcove. The women moved to intervene, but Liberty managed to stab all three, one after the other, before the dust settled and maybe before they even noticed we were in there. A growing pile of sandy corpses was gathering.

"The mechanics are fairly simple," Ethic said. "We have motorized toys you can buy in any market along the river. The full-sized versions require fuel though. You could only go so far before needing to refuel again. I suppose an armored mobile carriage could be a way to escape, but . . . "

Yellow asked, "But what?"

Liberty shushed us all. Before anyone could ask what was wrong, a spread of about a dozen or more figures walked past our hideout with the flow of the undead above. They parted and walked around the bodies Liberty had piled up outside. And they kept going.

She stuck her head out a little and looked both ways before

giving a thumbs up again. Those zombies must've fallen off the side of the slope farther back from our position and just kept walking.

How long was it going to be before they had us surrounded and pinned in?

Yellow repeated her question. "But what for?"

"Maybe to steer them, which might be why we're not getting anywhere," Ethic said. "Maybe they're just trying to escape the last town that got overrun and are sort of trapped in the midst of the horde, trying to find a way out."

"We don't have anything like that," Liberty said, with her eyes still set outside our shelter.

"What do you mean?" Ethic asked.

"We don't have anything like that," she repeated. "Any armored motorized carriages to escape these things. If we can't get them to herd away from the river, and hard away at that, then Dry Stretch is going to be gone and everyone with it, just like all the towns north this horde has overrun."

I wondered if she was starting to regret her no vote. I supposed it wouldn't have changed much if she had voted the other way.

"We'll need to make one more try," Ethic said. "We need to move them hard away. If there are people in the middle, motorized hiding spots or not, we might be doing them a favor if we can clear these monsters off. Can you move?"

I realized he was talking to me. "Yes."

"You'll need to keep up with us and be quick to follow commands, better at it than you were at obeying your father."

That stung. Stung more later. It was true, which was probably why. "I will."

"We'll have to get the horde going another way and then lead them off. Once we get out and ahead, we'll need to peel off quickly, to save our own skins and to keep from leading them home. Understood?"

I nodded.

We gathered our gear and weapons before we shuffled out into the open again. I moved quickly away from the slope. I didn't want any of those things tumbling down on my head. I was already breathing hard.

Liberty kept her eyes up on the droves of zombies marching along above us as she spoke to me. "Pace yourself, kid."

Ethic glanced at us and then back up at the monsters. "Everyone ready?"

None of the zombies seemed to notice us as they shuffled one foot in front of the other ever closer to Dry Stretch.

Ethic raised his rifle to the sky but angled it out over their heads. The bullet would probably carry all the way out over the river when he fired. I braced myself. He lowered his aim a little more. Not sure he was really aiming at all.

I was braced but still startled with the first shot. He fired five in a row. Four of the shots hit zombies in the sides of their heads, dropping them and tripping up the ones beside them. One missed a head but burst a zombie's shoulder, causing the arm to dangle from cords of flesh and ligament.

The horde turned and poured over the hill after us. They piled up high before the undead started to pick themselves loose from one another. The first few crawled after us. The next wave took to their feet and reached out for us as they stumbled forward. More poured over the side in pursuit.

Ethic reloaded as he said, "Wait a moment longer. We don't want to lose them."

I most definitely wanted to lose them.

He fired two more shots level into the oncoming crowd. He was more interested in the noise than in the impact. There was so much dust boiling up from all those bodies that I couldn't tell if he hit anything or not. It would have been hard to miss that mass of walking corpses.

"Let's move!"

I was deathly afraid my legs would betray me, that I would be locked in place in my terror. But I got moving just fine. The hard part was pacing myself as we marched along, leading the horde behind us.

We were in ruins, but nothing like the ones outside Dry Stretch. These were more spread out. Rock and dirt climbed up and clung to the shapes of structures and illegible signs. More of the ancient, motorized carriages sat within some of the ruins, on the edge of crumbling away entirely.

It made me think about our strangers motoring around among the horde. It made me wonder if there were ruins like these spread out everywhere all across the land. I thought about something Granby had said as I rode home with him after the full body votes.

I had questions, but we were busy with other things, and I knew the party was perturbed by my appearance in their business again, as they were busy trying to save everyone.

Ethic kept turning around. I watched his eyes looking for fear, but he just watched.

"Slow down," he said, and I wanted to scream.

My every muscle was tight as I listened to their moans and gravelly groans so close behind us. And their stink carried to us thick and raw as the wind turned against our backs.

Then, they started screaming. That's what I thought I was hearing. My soul could have left my body as every nerve end within me buzzed with terror. They were singing. It was a howling, warbling noise. It pierced the world. Then, it cut off abruptly, leaving my ears ringing with the muffled dull roll of their ordinary vocalizations. The wail started again just as before.

Ethic turned and walked backward. As he did, he cursed with a string of words, many of which I didn't know at the time, and I had heard plenty helping my father string wire for fence or repairing a stubborn section of the barn's roof high off the ground.

I expected there to be giants among the undead, maybe rotting creatures with wings like decomposing harpies swooping down onto us with their screams. When I lost my fight with temptation again and looked over my shoulder, it was just the ordinary zombies mobbing after us. It felt like far less than I thought were behind us, but they were still hideous and awful.

That siren blare whooped up and down a few more times, echoing shrill across the land. Facing it, I could tell it was much farther behind the zombies than I could see. I faced forward still not wanting to gaze upon those monsters.

"What is that clamor?" Liberty asked in the next lull.

"It's an unnatural sound," Ethic said.

"Surely so," agreed Yellow.

"That's not what I mean," he said. "It's being produced on purpose, but artificially, by something that is amplifying the sound so they all hear it."

"To what end?" Locust asked.

"To lead them away," Ethic said, "or rather back. To foil our plans to divert them from the path they are on."

"The one that will lead them to Dry Stretch and our families," I said.

"Now we know those souls in their motorized toys are against us for whatever reason," Yellow said.

I glanced back again. "They're still following us. It might still work, Ethic."

"There are only a couple hundred left. The rest have peeled away. We're doing this for nothing now."

"A couple hundred still feels like a lot to me," I said, and it did, but I knew the horde I had scanned through the glass were thousands strong, maybe innumerous.

"We don't have time to lead all these away and then come back," Ethic said. "The rest of the horde will be upon Dry Stretch with them all unaware and unprepared. We'll have to deal with these and then beat the horde home."

"How are we going to down two hundred zombies quickly without being eaten alive?" Yellow asked.

"What about there?" Locust pointed to a stone bridge ahead of us. "Across the gap."

I didn't understand what she meant.

"That might do fine," Ethic said. "Let's move."

We picked up the pace, and that was all I wanted. But then I saw what she meant by a gap. The roadway over the ancient bridge had collapsed not quite halfway across. The stone sides remained and the narrowest of ledges across.

Ethic held to the wall and shuffled along the drop off to one side. Bits of the ledge crumbled away under him. Liberty followed with no real sign of fear. Then, Locust.

"Are you freezing up on us?" Yellow asked me.

"I'm scared," I confessed.

"More than staying over here with them?"

I didn't bother to look again. I could hear them getting closer, and I never stopped smelling them. "I'm scared of both."

"We do what we must," Yellow said.

I was no more comforted, but we crossed over together feeling our footing coming loose the whole time. Once across, I stood farther back from the jagged edge of the road than the others.

They taunted and challenged the zombies. The undead crossed the bridge and continued toward us. A few in the front tried to stop, with some instinct to not step off an edge. The undead behind them kept coming and pushed each other off the drop in a wave. They bashed their heads open on the rocks far below.

A few actually tried to shuffle along the ledges to get over to us. I didn't like the idea that they had even that much intelligence. Liberty set up on one side to brain them when they got into range, and Ethic squared up on the other side. The zombies lost their balance and fell down after their fellows. The last couple broke most of their bones on impact, but a few didn't break open their heads due to the piles of cushioning flesh, only a couple though.

We had to cross the gap again. Now, if we fell, we would not only die but possibly be eaten alive as we expired. The ledge was breaking everywhere. We ended up crawling along the wall more than walking.

On the way back toward the path of the horde, we encountered a few more zombie stragglers still coming our way. The party took turns bringing them down and leaving them to rot in the forgotten street of these scant ruins. There were a couple clusters of three or four that had to be brought down one after the other, but nothing like the hundreds we lead to their fall and nothing like the horde still bearing down on our people.

"What's the plan?" Yellow asked. "Are we trying again?"

"No, there's no point, if they are being led along by bad agents within their numbers," Ethic said.

She followed up by asking, "Then, why are we walking back to them?"

Ethic said, "We're going to turn south at the next roadway. The vanguard of the horde is not that far ahead of our position now. It'll take some work, but we can get in front of them and then build up enough of a lead to get back in time to maybe—"

A gunshot echoed through the ruins, and we stopped. I found myself looking to the sky for some reason. The next three rounds landed close enough to kick up dust from the packed ground that hid the street.

Ethic pulled me sideways, and we all scrambled for cover. More shots hit the ruins and skipped along the ground near us.

The horde continued to move along, leaving us behind.

My father and Granby argued in the dark street across from the stables past the Hall. Others passed in both directions close enough to tell that an argument had ensued but not close enough to eavesdrop like they all wanted.

"What in the hell did you think you were doing in there?" my dad demanded very close to Granby's face. I swore he was going to hit the old man. Granby was tough, but he was still old.

"Telling the truth. What's got your cock in a knot, Bay?"

"Trying to stir the town up before we know all the facts."

"Wasn't a damned thing I said that wasn't fact. Resent you saying otherwise."

"As long as you live in my house, you can resent all you like and swallow it down."

"You going to threaten my stay in your house every time you hear something you don't like? Seems a childish way to be. Seems you can just get over it, especially since you got your way in the vote. Only thing worse than a sore loser is a bitter, angry winner."

"That's not the point, Granby."

"Not the point you care to hear, at least."

My father fumed. I wasn't sure what he intended to do. Wasn't quite sure why he was so upset with Granby. I just wanted it over.

"You carry ghost stories from a distant past that isn't relevant anymore. There aren't enough zombies left in the world to create a horde unless some idiot ran around gathering them. We don't need to make decisions that affect our livelihoods based on phantoms."

Granby sighed, and I thought he might relent, up until he said, "It takes less than you think to cluster those things up. And when the scouting party does come back with their report, we're going to have less time than you think to do anything about it. Maybe no more time than to run, leaving all behind, if we're lucky. That's my concern based on experience and not phantoms, Bay."

"I want to hear no more of it until we have real witness from the scouts."

Granby stepped away to collect his horse and buggy like he intended to do before my father waylaid him. "I said my piece in there, as is my damned right, you mule."

"Good enough," my father snapped back loud enough to echo.

Granby wasn't done. "But I don't give a goddamn what you want when it comes to my say, so don't misunderstand that."

Of course, that was the moment Minister Zink was passing by. She startled at Granby's curse and hustled along a little faster.

"Come along, boy," my father ordered.

The first of many fateful rebellions kicked in at that moment. "I want to ride back with Granby."

I expected a fight, maybe even a swat that my father had restrained from serving up to Granby himself. But he said, "Suit yourself."

Maybe that was the offhand decision that empowered me to disobey again and again following.

I ran after Granby to catch up.

15

We were only barely ahead of the horde as we reached Dry Stretch again and my family's land at its edge. There was already black smoke rising from the buildings.

I broke off in a full tilt up the path I had run with youthful joy so many times before and walked ever so slowly with dread other times. Ethic came with me even though he had every reason to continue on with his real business to the town proper.

He sent the other three instead. The women split with the road just beyond our land, each going for another point in the Stretch to spread the word as fast as possible.

I skid to a halt in the dooryard. There was an overturned vehicle, one of the motorized things, and its burning engine was the source of the smoke. Three bodies of strangers in rubber armor of their own lay twisted up and dead in the dirt. They appeared stabbed and shot. Wasn't sure which had killed them in the end.

The house was riddled with bullets. Windows shattered out. The door torn out of its frame and folded in half on the porch. Not sure how we didn't hear all this ruckus unless the moans of the dead behind us were that overwhelming.

We'd never sleep another night in that house again, it turned out.

A half dozen rotted corpses sprawled deeper in the property with their heads opened by blade and bullet. That made no sense with the horde still behind us.

More gunfire popped off. I thought it was the engine exploding, but the bullets tore out of the barn from the inside.

Ethic took his gun and ordered me to stay in cover behind the overturned metal. I disobeyed as I had done so much in this adventure.

A man in rubber armor fired into the barn again as he backed toward us. His armored vest looked much like the tire treads on the tipped vehicle out in the yard. Someone inside the barn fired back, and a modest squirt of blood spit out of a rupture in that rubber from the back of the man's shoulder.

Ethic took aim and moved to the side. The guy wore a helmet too. Don't know if it was bullet resistant, but it appeared Ethic was waiting for the guy to get closer before he took his shot.

I charged in screaming with my little work knife over my head. I think Ethic called my name, but I'm not positive on that.

The man started to turn, but I plunged my blade into his exposed neck between the top of his armor and the bottom edge of his helmet. He kept turning, and that tore open his neck in a nasty wound as he pulled himself off my knife. He dropped his gun at his feet but still tried to aim on me with his empty hands as he fell dead into the dirt and moldy straw.

It was the first taste of blood that knife got, but not the last. It was the first time I killed anyone, but not the last.

I saw Granby with his gun shaking in his hand. Then, I saw my dad on his back against the far wall. He gasped for air but couldn't seem to draw any as he drooled pink and red into his whiskers. He must have just missed shaving that morning. Bubbles grew and popped from the wounds in his chest. He was leaking from multiple holes.

I ran to his side, but his eyes focused on nothing.

Granby seemed more interested in the horses.

My father reached out one shaking hand and waved for Ethic to come to his side. He acted like he didn't see me at all. Ethic came.

Granby saddled up three of the horses in their stalls in a hurry.

My father pulled Ethic toward him with one bloody hand. Ethic turned his ear to my father's lips. There was a pause, and then my father exhaled his dying breath into the side of Ethic's face.

Granby opened the other stalls and hustled the other horses out, setting them to run free.

I knew the answer, but I asked anyway. "What'd he say?"

Ethic shook his head. "Nothing."

I wiped my tears as I stood on shaky legs. "Where's Mom? King, Kip, and Knoll?"

Granby was leading our last three horses out by their reins.

I yelled, "Answer me! Where are they?"

"Your mom took the boys to the tower."

It took me a beat to understand what he was saying. "They can't climb that. It's dangerous."

"They don't have to climb it as high as you," he said, "but they can get up one concrete floor above whatever is coming."

But there were stairs to the lowest level. Stairs!

"A lot more zombies are coming than what was in the yard here," Ethic said. He turned to me. "I'm sorry about your father."

I tried to swallow down my sorrow as it burned my throat. "There are more of these men leading and guiding the undead too."

"Then, we need to go," Granby handed off the reins of two of the horses to us.

"What about his body?" I asked.

"No time to bury him. I'm sorry," Granby said.

"Then, we should bring him," I cried.

Ethic mounted up. "Too much weight. You know how close they are behind us."

Granby climbed stiffly into the saddle, and I got on with less trouble. "They'll eat him. The zombies will eat him."

"We have other people to keep from getting eaten," Granby said. "The smoke is going to draw them here. We have to go now."

Before we were out to the road again, the first lines of the endless dead topped the horizon and seemed to stretch from the river into infinity. More and more lines rose into view.

I listened for the motors but heard none yet.

Ethic rode ahead of us and turned toward town. He must have known we had a different destination.

Granby and I crossed the road and raced through the fields beyond at a full gallop over the rolling hills sideways to the approaching threat.

"My ass is too bony to employ a horse without the buggy," he complained.

I think I intended to respond, but as we topped the next grassy hill, a wash of bodies rambled through the dip all across our path. More than a thousand just in that little contour of land trailing back into the mass of the horde and leading several yards ahead into Dry Stretch.

As our horses twisted from side to side under us, endeavoring to back away from the awful stench, more than a few of those monsters spied us and started trudging up the hill in our direction.

It appeared the horde was not moving in uniform fronts.

We turned our horses south, and they fled willingly toward town.

"I'm sure they reached the tower and are safe on the raised platform," Granby called out. "That fight in the yard went on a while and gave them a hell of a lead. Your father fought hard. Took down most of the bastards himself. He sacrificed himself to save them, and your mom will save them and herself."

Again, before I could answer, the threat interrupted. The shots roared off behind us and bullets ripped through the tall grasses on both sides of us. We pushed our horses a little harder.

I heard the motors then.

16

"Because he don't want it to be true," Granby answered me as we rode back in the dark in the light buggy from the full body. "None of them do."

"They shouldn't want to get eaten either," I said with my arms crossed.

Granby actually chuckled at me. He broke into coughing that took a moment to subside.

"Well," he started once he had himself back under control. "The scouts will come back with the report, and there won't be any denying what needs to be done then . . . maybe."

"What do you mean by maybe, Granby?"

"Well, folks can deny most any little thing if they're determined enough to have their way. Even in the face of all the evidence. It's just how we're strung together sometimes."

"How bad can it get?"

"What do you mean?"

I tried to think what I was asking. "How bad can the zombies get if they're in a horde?"

Granby whistled. The horse started to pull up, but he snapped the reins to keep it moving, letting the animal know that whistle wasn't for him. "Bad. It can get real bad. As bad as you can imagine. Worse than you can imagine actually. Millions of ruins out there, and all those people died. A lot of them rose after."

"Will it be the end of us?"

He thought a moment before answering, and I didn't like that. "Well, the worst it can get and the worst it's going to get this time are not necessarily one and the same. No matter how we voted tonight, we do have some forewarning. We are sending out scouts, which is the right thing to do. Some folks will prepare anyhow. The rest will catch up. Zombies can be led aside as well."

"Led aside?"

Granby chuckled again and managed not to cough this time. "The piece Ethic isn't telling anyone is that he plans to find the horde and guide it off track from Dry Stretch, lead it out into the barrens far from the river and us. Lose them out there and let them break up far from anyone they can hurt."

"He told you this?"

"Doesn't have to. He knows zombies. Deals with them all the time so the rest of us don't have to. If it was just scouting, he could go alone. Funny thing is, if he's successful, even with the witness of the rest of the party, no one will believe it was as bad as it could have been. No one will believe we were ever in that much danger."

I sighed and looked away. "That's not fair. People need to know he was right."

"Well, the price of being heroes is that people don't always get shown you were right, not completely. But make no mistake, everyone who goes out with Ethic to deal with this thing is as great a hero as Dry Stretch is ever going to see."

We talked about more on the way home, but that last bit stuck with me.

17

We rode into town, and the dead shambled down the road right behind us. People barricaded between two buildings across the street. The walls and fences around town were still in disrepair though. Townsfolk with guns lined up on the barricade to pick off the dead as they came. Others with long makeshift spears lined up behind them.

Then, the horde emerged and spread across the land in both directions wider than the town itself. Everyone exchanged looks but held their ground. I think they knew their plan was hopeless, but they had a duty.

Then, a motor revved. A vehicle tore through and out of the undead crowd, breaking and scattering zombies in its path. The armored hulk barreled on ahead. It had done us no favors with the few zombies it had taken down as it picked up speed. I don't think the others knew what to make of it as it closed in on them and they stood frozen.

"Run!" I yelled from the back of my horse deeper in town.

Everyone scattered as the metal thing blasted through the barrier, sending scrap flying everywhere.

"Ride!" Granby cried, and we set off galloping through town on horses already lathered with sweat.

Gunfire peppered the buildings around us. People screamed. My horse reared, and I almost held on before it dumped me and ran off.

I landed hard on a section of road that still had paving cobbles. Tore myself up and lay there a couple beats in shock. I was lucky not to break anything, especially my neck.

I heard the motor tearing toward me. It took all my will to roll to the side over and over. A blade scraped the ground through where I had first landed, throwing sparks off the old cobbles.

I met eyes with the man who had leaned out the open door to cut me up on the run. He stuck out his tongue at me and slammed the door again.

The first zombies walked over the leveled barrier at the end of the main street. I knew others were already slipping through holes in the fences and through alleys all along the northern side of town. That was how the horde worked.

I lumbered to my feet, feeling as stiff as Granby. He was nowhere to be found. I limped my way up a side street. I wanted to get out of town, but I knew my best bet was to find my way to one of the roofs. There were ladders on some of the buildings further down.

People ran all around me.

A zombie missing one side of its face but still snapping all its teeth together staggered out in our midst. It came for me as I limped wide around it and did my best to stay ahead. A woman carrying a small child ran past me not looking. She bumped right into the zombie, and it almost grabbed her, but she kept going, never making eye contact with it. The snapping monster turned away from me and followed her.

A gunshot blasted right next to me, and I startled. A man fell to his back, and the weapon he'd just used skidded away along the packed dirt surface. A zombie fell on top of him and sunk its teeth into his neck.

I pulled my knife and drove it into the creature's ear. It took an effort to pull the blade loose again, and the dead weight of the corpse rolled off, revealing the man bleeding out dark from his ruined neck. He reached for me, gagging and choking, "End it. End it. Please . . . "

I knew what he was asking, but I couldn't do it. I moved around him and kept going. I knew he'd die, and I knew he'd turn into a zombie after, but I couldn't do it.

My father had been unable to get off any last words, and I wondered if that was a blessing.

More zombies poured out from where the first had come and fell on the body of the bleeding man. He screamed for a long time.

A group of armed townsfolk fleeing the other way bumped into me and sent me sprawling. My knife skipped away from me. I crawled toward it, and a girl not much older than me stepped on my hand as she ran by. I cried out and then kept crawling.

As I got a hand on my knife, another disfigured woman got her teeth on me, crawling in from the side. I pulled my hand away. I felt the teeth but didn't appear to have a mark. You never could tell though. She kept coming for another bite.

I stabbed her through the eye but didn't quite get the brain until I twisted the blade around inside her head a couple times. She finally went down. Even more came out behind her, and I started running despite the pain in my skinned knees.

After a little while, I stopped short. Two more vehicles sat outside the stores, and armored men ran back and forth from inside loading up goods they were looting. I was starting to get a picture of the game they were playing with the horde and the towns. I just couldn't believe anyone would do that to other people.

The men were laughing and shooting up at the taller buildings around.

Someone grabbed my shirt and pulled me backward. I twisted away and saw a naked woman leaking green rot from a dozen different wounds. I stabbed through her ear and scuttled away as she fell. Too many more to take on myself followed her, so I was forced to run toward the shooting.

The men broke off to go back into the stores, so I made to run past them while I had the chance. I stopped again though as I saw Ethic and Locust run out across the street. They tossed a glass bottle each into the open vehicles and retreated.

Cold fingers brushed my back, and I ran too. I was starting to pass the vehicles when Ethic grabbed me and pulled me sideways through the door of the building across the street. The explosions followed one after the other, folding the metal open as it set ablaze. Windows shattered in the buildings around them.

Another vehicle motored toward our position along another street. Locust opened a window that still had glass. She lit a fuse and tossed it onto the hood of the vehicle as it buzzed by. It bounced around as the vehicle slowed, and then the explosion washed fire inside and out. The men rolled out swallowed in fire themselves. I thought of my father as I watched them burn.

Yet another pulled up, and the men stepped out with weapons. We ducked away as they shot inside at us.

Locust got ready to light another bomb when more gunfire erupted, and the armored men started falling.

We raised up to see Granby and several women marching down the street with their weapons at the ready. Aleo was among them. They passed our position and started shooting the zombies out in the street beyond the burning vehicles and men.

I ran out and tried to follow Granby, but I was grabbed around the throat. A bleeding man in rubber armor held a gun to the side of my head.

Ethic rose up and fired twice high. I think he was afraid of hitting me.

The guy turned his gun away from me and onto Ethic in the building. He suddenly jerked backward, losing his grip on me and the gun. Yellow dragged him down to the dirt with a chain wrapped around his neck from behind. He clawed at his throat and then reached for his weapon nearby. I kicked the gun further away along the ground as Ethic and Locust came out.

Locust prepared to light another glass bomb, but Yellow said, "No, wait. We can use it."

The guy continued to choke as I picked up his gun and made it my own.

"Use it how?" Locust asked.

"We can run down the other vehicles faster," she said, "and lead the zombies away just as they led them here."

The guy was still choking. It was going to take a while to finish strangling him.

"God, that's smart," Ethic said.

Yellow stood up, braced her boot on the man's shoulder, and twisted hard to the side three times. His neck snapped the last time.

We piled in with the containers of the remaining bombs, some juiced-up version of the stuff some ranches used to blow up gopher holes, and Ethic tried to steer the rumbling machine. We ran up on curbs and scraped the walls as we went.

"Hold it steady," Locust ordered. "This stuff is volatile."

"I'm trying," he grumbled.

"Try harder," Yellow said.

Another vehicle passed in front of us, and Ethic turned after it. It was long, large, and heavy, so we were able to catch up alongside it. There was a big bell like a horn attached to the top. Locust opened the door. For some reason, a man in the other vehicle opened his. Maybe he thought one of his buddies wanted to talk.

She lit the fuse and tossed the bomb inside past him. They scrambled around as we veered away. I spied zombies chained up in there with them, like the ones set loose at my family's farm. I leaned out to get a better look. They ran off the road and up a wall, almost flipping over before they blew apart.

I heard one crackling squawk of sound that reminded me of the siren from earlier, but then it was gone.

I met eyes with Aleo and some of the others as we sped away. I think I got more credit for fighting off the bastards than I deserved.

We raced out of town. I'd never gone all the way through town so fast.

"Where are we going?" Yellow asked.

I was focused on how many more undead were wandering out there in the open. Too many.

"I hope they'll follow us to the river. Maybe we can wash them away," Ethic said. "Save ourselves and the towns south too."

With the door still open, I got Locust to light one, and I rolled another bomb even with no vehicles around. One of the zombies actually reached down to pick it up. The explosion lifted several of them twirling apart in the air.

A few more of those and the horde really was after us.

I kept expecting a siren to foil our plans, but that device remained silent.

18

My mom tucked me in after I returned in Granby's buggy from the full body. It was odd because she seldom did anymore.

"Your father isn't mad. He's just concerned."

The fact she came to tell me this meant he was really mad. I had other things on my mind though.

"What if the zombies do come though?"

"We'll deal with it." She patted my head.

I pressed the point. "But if it's a horde . . . "

My voice sounded smaller, younger than I was.

"We'll deal with it. We'll survive it. Worry solves nothing. Sleep is important though. Your father and I will let nothing happen to you and your brothers. I swear it."

She kissed my forehead and left me in the dark.

19

Ahead of us, Glorigold, Liberty, and other hands fought off a small cluster of zombies trying to get at them and the herds. We buzzed past with the horde behind us. They watched us come and then turned to fight the new wave of undead.

The dead swept over Liberty and some of the others. Glorigold fled. Her herds were devoured. I told myself Liberty could have escaped, but I found out later she had not.

We did her wrong that day.

We neared the river beyond Glorigold's land.

A sleek vehicle struck us from the side and rolled us. The glass bombs scattered everywhere. Ethic forced open the door and all four of us bailed out.

Our attackers turned again to run us down. Locust retrieved a bomb, lit it, and threw. They dodged and it exploded.

The dead were still coming.

She threw another; they dodged again.

Yellow lit one and rolled it not far away as the vehicle kept coming. "Run!"

We did.

The man with his tongue out leaned from the door with his blade again. It exploded under them and lifted them into the air. Our vehicle rolled behind us as we ran toward the oncoming horde. The other bombs exploded, enveloping our car, and Yellow too.

She was just gone. No trace.

We stopped and ran toward the river again.

We reached the bank and then had to wade out. The dead pushed each other into the water like they'd done over the bridge and washed downstream with us.

Making it ashore, we hid in the brush. I could see the tower on the other side of the endless zombies. It was hours before they all passed, and I ran.

I arrived to find piles of dead bodies under the tower. More zombies milled around. My brothers cried from the floor above. I started stabbing corpses in their heads. Ethic and Locust took out the others. I didn't realize they were with me.

My brothers cried for my mother. I started rolling the bodies away and found her at the bottom. Alive, but barely. She was bitten many times more than the messenger had been. I hated my brothers for not coming down to help her. She had killed many of them on her own, until she was buried in them, at the base of the stairs, protecting her sons as she'd promised.

"Take care of your brothers." Her eyes rolled up in her head.

I used the stolen gun to shoot her and then used my knife to be sure she wasn't coming back.

Glorigold arrived with some of her people and punched Ethic in the face. Her own ranch hands had to pull her off.

I ignored them as I helped my brothers down.

Granby came and sobbed over his granddaughter. "Winn! Winn! My dear Winn!"

20

Glorigold wanted Ethic tried for bringing the horde over her land. It didn't go anywhere. She had very little power left at the time, losing everything. She built back, acquiring land from other dead farmers, owning more than she did before. She even served as mayor for a while. Ethic beat her in the next election, and then she beat him to take it back. The women who lead now weren't even alive during all this.

The towns south did have some trouble with a river full of zombies, but not as much as they would have. Didn't learn much about the bastards who led the horde. Not sure if we killed them all either.

With Granby's help, I ran the farm that was mine now by right. We tore down the house and built a new one. My brothers married and built houses of their own on the land we worked together.

The zombies didn't find my father's body in the barn, so we were able to bury him and my mother beside each other up on the hill over there in the family plot.

Glorigold died with no heirs, so all her land was split up for sale. We got some of it, and that's why our farm is the largest holding across the whole north of Dry Stretch—that and me marrying Aleo with all her land, of course.

Ethic Hanover is long dead now, but I learned from him and kept up his work. It's why I go out in the ruins and keep the zombies thin while you, your parents, and your cousins keep up the land.

This land will be yours one day, but so will the responsibility of the undead.

I will never forget what they can become, and we must not allow them to gather in numbers against us ever again. Never again.

So, take up your weapons and come with me, my granddaughters. There is work to be done.

ZOMBIE DINER

ARMAND ROSAMILIA

1

GRADY HARPER WONDERED if the waitress was even wearing underwear. *Probably something frilly, or maybe a thong,* he thought and smiled to himself.

Louise squeezed his leg under the table and leaned close to him. "One more time you stare at that little whore's ass, and I'm leaving."

Grady ignored his wife and went back to his coffee, which was getting cold. He raised his hand to get the waitress's attention but thought better of it. *Better leave that well enough alone for now.* "I'm going to the bathroom."

"Not alone," his wife hissed. She turned to their son, Drew. "Go with your father to the bathroom."

Drew grimaced and looked to his younger sister, Isabella, for help. She ignored her family, head down in her plate of pancakes. "Fine," he finally said. "Izzy is coming with me."

"Stop calling her that; you know she hates it."

Drew smiled. "Don't care." He crossed his arms. "If Izzy isn't going, I'm not going."

Grady leaned over and was glad he was in public, or he'd probably lose it on these two little ingrates. "Both of you get up and follow me. Now."

The diner was packed. Grady fought his way past the main entrance, where thirty people were lined up. The hostess, a young gal with pretty eyes and pert boobs, smiled wanly at him.

"What, are you giving away free food?" he said with a laugh to her.

She shook her head. "They said on the radio they're closing I-10 down."

"Seriously?"

"We were trying to get back to Louisiana, but the cops blocked it off. We had to turn back," an older gentleman said from in line. A few others piped in, talking about other major roads being closed coming south and north.

As if on cue a police car, sirens roaring, sped past them outside.

Grady rubbed his temples and went to the bathroom, but there were at least six people in line waiting their turn. He tussled Drew's hair, even though he was sixteen and hated it. The boy was almost as tall as Grady and a spitting image of his mom. *Same attitude as well.*

He turned to his fifteen-year-old daughter and sighed. She also looked like Louise and had the same attitude and hatred toward him, mostly ignoring him. She was supposed to have been daddy's little girl but somewhere, a long time ago, she decided to side with mommy and gang up on him. Even he liked calling her Izzy and pissing her off, using the excuse that he'd always called her that from the time she was a baby and it was cute.

A dad came out of the bathroom with two small children in tow, both wearing black mouse ears. As if reading his mind, Drew spoke up. "When we get there, I'm not wearing those stupid baby things."

"Your sister will."

"Doubt it," Drew said and pulled out his cell phone, leaning against the wall.

Drew was right. With his son, he could at least plead and beg and make a joke out of it until Drew would reluctantly put the damn things on. Isabella? No fucking way.

This trip to Orlando was supposed to have been fun and a bonding experience for the family, especially after Grady's affair. *Affairs,* he thought, *but she only knows about the one.* Just as well. If Louise ever found out about her brother's wife or Stephanie from the bank, she'd leave him for sure. Not to mention the next-door neighbor, June . . .

He hadn't wanted to stop. They were only a couple of hours from Orlando and had just gotten into Florida. But the kids were hungry and the wife was bitchy and he needed a break.

As people crowded into the diner, he was amazed that, when they'd gotten here forty minutes ago, the place was half-empty. Now it was wall-to-wall customers.

An ambulance, followed by a fire truck, went by outside. Everyone in line turned and stared.

"The news just said there's some huge accident or something in Georgia," someone in line said.

"My cousin in Atlanta said they're closing the city up. He just posted on Facebook."

"Time to go," Grady said to his son. He had a bad feeling about this . . . whatever this was.

By the time he got back to the table, a fist-fight had broken out in a corner, probably over a seat. Louise stared at him with contempt. "What took so long? Did you con the waitress into a stall with you?"

Grady ignored her taunt. "We need to leave."

"I'm not done," she said.

As the noise level rose in time with Grady's pounding headache, he grabbed her plate of food and smashed it on the floor. No one seemed to notice. "We are leaving. Let's go."

The Harper family pushed through the crowd.

Grady caught a last glimpse of the waitress and sighed. She did have a great ass.

"What's going on?" Louise said as they got to the mini-van.

"I'm not sure." Grady opened the doors with the key just as a fireball rose from the north, followed by more sirens.

They piled into the car, but Grady didn't start it.

"What's wrong? You rush us to leave, throw my food on the table, don't pay for dinner, and now we're waiting for what? The cops over there to arrest us?" Louise smacked the dashboard.

Grady had his stare fixed on the other side of the busy road. "What are they doing?" he finally asked, transfixed.

"The homeless people? Who cares. Can we go?"

He couldn't quite put his finger on what was odd about the group. There were four of them, dirty and covered in something. One was on the ground and seemed to be fighting off the others, but then that one stopped struggling and all four stood.

"What's on them?" Drew said from the backseat. "Is that blood?"

"No way. They'd be dead if they lost that much blood," Louise said calmly.

Grady felt like they were watching a movie with disinterest.

"Those are the idiots who do the zombie walks. I saw it on G4. I think there's one in Jacksonville this weekend," Isabella chimed in.

Grady was about to make a snappy comment about her first words spoken in the car the entire trip when one of the 'homeless people/zombie walkers' moved straight into traffic and promptly got run over.

"Holy mother of God!" Louise said. "Did you see that?"

Stifling down another snappy comment, Grady got out of the car. "What the fuck is going on?"

Before the body was done flying through the air, the other three members of the entourage also stepped into the street and were hit.

A car behind the initial accident tried to steer away and ended up slamming sideways into two cars.

"Are they drunk?" Grady asked, but no one else from his family had gotten out of the car. He turned back to the diner at the sound of noise, but they were parked nearer the street, and he couldn't get a good look as to what was happening. He imagined it wasn't good.

This entire day was going to shit. He glanced at his wife in the front seat and smiled at her, but she looked away. *Bitch.*

Screams brought his attention back to the street. The initial victim, pinned under the front end of a car, was actually biting the woman trying to help him.

"He's biting her," Grady said in astonishment. The other victims were engaged in the same bizarre behavior, chaos erupting. As people were bitten they screamed and ran, but some were being pulled down to the ground or being hit by other cars, trying to escape.

Louise finally stepped out of the car and joined her husband. "Are you going to stare at the car accident? We need to leave before they close this off."

"Seriously?" He wanted to punch her in the face. "Do you see what's going on?"

"Car accident," she said but put her hand to her mouth. "Grady, what are those people doing?"

"Biting people."

"We need to leave."

Grady watched as a woman, face dripping blood, locked dead eyes on him and began walking across the street. *This isn't really happening; this is part of the zombie thing from Jacksonville, people on their way home and still fucking around.*

"Maybe they're shooting a movie or one of those *CSI: Miami* episodes."

"I don't see cameras or a production crew," Louise said. "We need to get out of here."

They got back in the mini-van, and Grady locked the doors, feeling instantly safer when he heard the click.

"What's going on?" Drew asked.

Louise turned to her son with a big, fake smile. "Nothing, honey, everything is great."

Grady hated when she talked to the kids like they were still six. He didn't think bringing it up right now would be the right time and knew there was never going to be a right time. "Everything is an argument," he whispered.

"Did you say something?"

"No." Grady looked out the window. The woman had made it across the street and was on the sidewalk and still heading their way.

"What's wrong with that lady?" Isabella asked from the backseat, actually taking her headphones off. "She looks sick or something."

Louise gripped Grady's arm. *Wow, all it takes is a car accident and bloody people for her to touch me,* he wanted to say but wisely thought instead.

Another ambulance shot past, ignoring the scene right here, right now. Grady wondered what could be worse than this accident but decided he didn't want to know.

"We need to go," Louise said and squeezed his arm.

Grady was drawn to the muffled sounds of gunfire through the closed windows, but he didn't know if they were coming from the diner or nearby. He assumed they were guns firing since he'd never actually been around one. Sure, he'd seen plenty of cool action movies at the theatre, in surround sound, and marveled at watching Matt Damon or Bruce Willis shooting a dozen bad guys like it was nothing. Last weekend Grady had slept on the couch and watched a crime movie starring Ben Affleck that he loved, and that had cops and bank robbers shooting it out near Fenway Park.

The woman, her nose and left ear bloody clumps of meat, slammed her head against his side door and brought him back from his daydreaming.

Grady stared at her and wondered who she was—who she had

been—and what was now going through that head of hers. This close he had no doubt she was dead if that made any sense.

She banged her head with such force against his window that it rattled, and he was sure it would shatter, shards of glass raining down on his lap.

Louise punched him in the arm and began screaming, words jumbled but the message was clear.

Grady turned the mini-van on and calmly put it in drive, proud that he didn't panic like in those horror movies he wasn't allowed to watch anymore.

The woman thumped against the side as they moved, but Grady couldn't get to the main road from this side of the parking lot. There seemed to be something big and bad going on right outside the diner now.

"I can't get onto the highway," he finally said. A glance in his side mirror confirmed that the dead woman was making her way toward them. "The accident might block us in anyway."

"We need to get out of here," Louise said, and Grady could tell she'd caught sight of the woman in her mirror. "Drive around the back."

He didn't want to drive too fast with so much going on around him, but when someone stepped out to his left he instinctively jammed his foot on the gas and sped off, nearly hitting the guy. He looked alive to Grady, but he didn't know how long that would last with the dead woman coming up the row.

"What if there isn't a way out back there?" he asked.

No one answered his question as they raced around, the building to their left and more cars parked to their right with a high wooden fence separating this lot from the next.

There was another parking lot behind the diner, and it was packed, with the outside rows double-parked and not passable.

"Watch out!" Louise yelled.

Grady slammed on the brakes and came within inches of hitting a man, who screamed in fright and put his hands up.

"Is everyone alright?" Grady asked.

No one answered, but he knew they were fine. It was one of those parental things you had to say during an accident or close call. *A recognition of some sort would have been good, and it wouldn't have fucking killed you,* he thought as he stared at his wife.

The guy recovered, stomped to Grady's door, and calmly tapped on the window. He was dark-skinned with curly black hair and bright, blue eyes.

"Drive," his wife said.

He didn't know if it was a hunch, fate, or just him giving the old Fuck You to Louise, but instead of obeying her command, he rolled down the window.

"Open the door and let me in."

"Huh?" Grady said dumbly.

The guy looked pissed. "There's all Hell breaking loose in there, and we need to get going. I live close to here; I need to get my family. Let me in."

Louise shook her head and stared at her husband.

Again, Grady had no real control. *You don't push Grady Harper, not today, bitch, not ever again.* He unlocked the door, and the guy ran around and jumped in.

"Is there a way out the back?" Grady asked.

"If you want to crash through the back fence. It's only wood, and it takes you to the side street and away from this place," he said. "I'm P.C., by the way. I'm the head chef there."

"P.C.?" Drew asked.

The man smiled, showing two gold teeth. "My grandma called me Pork Chop when I was a kid growing up in Alabama. It just stuck. Much better than Charlie, I think."

Grady stopped the mini-van at the end of the aisle, pointing the car at the wooden fence. Even with the windows up, they could hear gunshots.

"Fuck it," Grady mumbled and backed up.

"Where are you going?" Louise asked, with anger in her voice.

"Running start," Pork Chop said with a laugh. "Punch it."

Grady stopped and put it in drive just as the sound of screams came from the parking lot area to their right.

"Punch it," he said quietly and floored the mini-van, aiming at the fence.

2

Pork Chop pointed at the house and smiled. "Number twelve, that's me."

Grady had driven only three blocks through a winding development of unassuming houses, all dropped onto manicured lawns in neat little rows. With the sun going down you could imagine the scene at the diner being a dream or a movie. The lights were on in most houses, streetlights flaring, and an old man stood across the street watering his lawn.

"Come on in and meet my old lady," Pork Chop said.

As they exited the mini-van, Louise stopped. "You hear that?"

At first, Grady didn't know what she was talking about, but then he heard it, like an insect buzzing: a cacophony of sirens, all blending in the distance. *This is something huge and scary.* He wondered if they'd ever get home.

"Nice place," Louise said simply.

"Thanks. Me and Camille bought it in the early nineties before the economy turned sour. We're thinking of putting a pool out back next summer." He used his key to open the front door. "Camille? We have guests. You decent?"

A striking black woman, older than Pork Chop, came into view. She looked positively annoyed. "Why are you home so soon?"

"People eating people at the diner. Don't you have the news on?"

"No, I'm watching my shows. Who are these people in my house?"

Pork Chop put his hands up and approached her like a cornered animal.

Grady could see who wore the pants in this family, and he sighed. It was the same in his. Despite what was going on, he also couldn't help but notice that Camille was quite attractive, with big brown eyes under frizzy hair and an hourglass body. He'd never slept with a black woman before, but they were at the top of his list, right under Asian chicks.

They spoke quietly and heatedly. Camille glanced at them and smiled, deferring to Louise. "I'll put some coffee on, and Pork Chop will show you to the living room and the television." She walked away quickly.

The living room was spacious, with off-white walls and dark wood trim. A glass display case held dozens of varied fairy statuettes. A large, ornate bookcase took up one wall, and it was overflowing with books, most of them rather large and about art.

Pork Chop let them take all the seats around the coffee table and grabbed the remote, turning on the cable company's local news.

"Don't turn off *Friends*. I haven't seen that one before," Camilla yelled from the kitchen.

"Oh my sweet God," Pork Chop said and dropped the remote control on the floor.

At first, it was hard to see what exactly was going on because the camera was at an angle and low. When the talking head newscaster, tiny at the bottom right corner of the screen, began gasping instead of reporting, they all followed suit.

"That must have been a cameraman," Drew said. "Wow."

The picture cut to an aerial view of Jacksonville. It was like watching a war movie, with buildings on fire and smoke blocking part of the scene.

"Look at all the people down there," Grady said but then almost covered his eyes when the camera tightened the shot and the horde of people were all dead like the people outside the diner.

"Reports coming in confirm that people are actually biting other people . . . is this a joke?" the newscaster asked, clearly shaken. "A report on the AP is saying New York, Chicago, Los Angeles, Dallas, and Atlanta are under siege, and the respective governors have declared martial law. This is unreal."

Grady turned to see Camilla, face stricken, leaning against the door jam. "Is this some kind of hoax?" she asked.

"I don't think so." Pork Chop went to her and hugged his wife. "We need to secure the house."

Grady wanted to jump in and start giving orders, giving everyone a task, and keeping them busy so no one panicked. A true leader would grin and get the house looking like a fortress in an hour.

Instead, he sat on the couch and couldn't move, watching a live shot on the television from Philadelphia. Three dead people were ripping an old man apart.

"If I'd known it was crazy all over I would've grabbed some food from the diner," Pork Chop said. He turned to Grady. We need to get some supplies before everyone panics and starts looting. Do you have a gun?"

Louise snorted but was quiet when Grady looked at her. He was sure she was going to make some comment about his manliness and how he'd be afraid to carry a gun or own one.

Grady shook his head and glanced at his wife, wishing he had one because right now, as embarrassed as he was, he fantasized about putting the barrel of it in her mouth and painting the wall behind her red. *Jesus Christ, what's wrong with me?* he thought.

Pork Chop was pacing now. "Alright, the men will drive over to the Publix on Clark Street and see if we can gather some food while the women start fortifying the house. Sound like a plan?"

"No." Camille and Louise both said at the same time.

Louise stepped forward. "What do you expect us to do, start hammering two-by-fours over the windows?"

Grady didn't bother correcting her.

"Can I talk to you for a second? Now?" Camille said to her husband, anger on her face.

"Excuse us one second," Pork Chop said and followed his wife down the hall.

"We need to leave," Louise said. "We need to get home."

Grady pointed at the flashing news on the television. "Every major road is jammed with cars, the big cities are under attack— including ours, by the way—and people are clearly insane and eating one another. I think the best thing to do is to hole up here until the Army or National Guard clears the streets and restores order."

Drew came up and stood next to his dad, clearly freaked out. "I want to go home."

Louise looked at her son and put a hand gently on his chin. She turned to her husband. "I'll go with the cook to the store while you and the kids and his bitchy wife get this place secured."

"I'm coming with you, mom," Drew said.

"I need you here to help." Grady turned to his daughter, who was staring blankly at the television. "I think Isabella needs to get away from that for a bit."

Pork Chop and Camille came back into the living room. "Change of plans," Pork Chop said. "I'll take your wife and one of the kids to the store."

Louise smiled and looked at Camille. "Great minds think alike.

I'm Louise, by the way, and this is my son Drew and his sister Isabella." She glanced at Grady. "He's Grady. We're so sorry to intrude on your nice home like this, but it is nuts out there right now."

Camille put on a fake smile. "Not a problem. I'm just hoping we can get through this quickly and get on with our normal, boring lives." She turned to Grady. "P.C. has his tools in the garage, and there's an old shed out back that we can use for wood. If that's not enough, the neighbor next door isn't home. They use that place as a winter home, so we could use it if we have to."

Grady smiled. "Come on, Drew, let's get going." He turned to Louise. "Be careful."

Louise ignored her husband and put out her hand. "I need the car keys."

Pork Chop needed a drink, a stiff double shot of whiskey to ease his nerves. Of course, that wouldn't really solve anything other than the shakes he felt coming on.

He glanced at the woman next to him in the passenger seat and smiled, but she ignored him. The daughter was crashed on the backseat, headphones on, like it was a typical shitty day out with the parents.

Driving away from the diner, it was like moving back into the real world. There were no people killing people, no fires and sirens and death, only normal traffic coming and going.

The radio stations were all broadcasting live from trouble spots, but most people in their cars were listening to Spotify or downloaded songs instead of the radio. "It's a lost art," Pork Chop mumbled to himself. He'd been a communication major in college with his eye on being a radio DJ, but bad grades and drinking had derailed him. The drinking had derailed most of his dreams.

He pulled into the supermarket parking lot, expecting to see a madhouse. Instead, it was busy, but people were smiling and going about their business.

"They have no idea what's happening," Louise said. "Look at them, going about their business."

"A mile away people are biting people," Pork Chop said as he exited the mini-van. "We need to make this quick before someone catches on."

At Louise's suggestion, they each grabbed a shopping cart. "Let's do this intelligently. I'll start at this end, Pork Chop that way. Isabella, go to the meat section and fill your cart with as much as you can."

"Who's going to pay for that?" her daughter asked.

"I have my credit card, but if the world keeps moving in this direction, I doubt I'll have to pay the bill when it comes in."

Pork Chop went to the deli and put every pre-packaged meat and cheese item into his cart, ignoring some stares. The juice aisle was behind him, and he randomly selected twenty bottles. He decided against fresh fruit and vegetables since they'd go bad eventually.

The next aisle was soup, and he topped off the shopping cart with as varied a selection as he could but as quickly as he could.

Pork Chop got into line at the checkout and was annoyed at how slow the cashier was working, chit-chatting with an elderly woman in line.

He glanced around and waved when he saw Louise and her daughter already in line and putting their items on the moving belt.

Pork Chop idly tossed some of the candy bars and other impulse items onto his pile while he waited for the old woman to finally move.

By the time he got through the line, swiped his card, paid for his four-hundred and sixty-two-dollar purchase, and made it outside, Louise and her daughter were already loading the van.

He parked his shopping cart next to them and nodded. "I'm going back in."

"We'll load up and join you," Louise said. "So far so good."

Pork Chop hooked another cart and made his way to the cleaning aisle, figuring they needed other supplies besides food. He added bottles of bleach, sponges, and various cleaners before finishing with toilet paper and paper towels.

He decided he was going to fill as many carts as he could until the mini-van was packed solid, rush home, and have everyone help unload before coming back again.

Pork Chop was swiping his other Visa card when he heard a scream. He turned to see two men fighting over a bulk package of tissues.

"What's gotten into them?" the cashier asked.

"I don't know. Can we please hurry?" He had a bad feeling about this.

The noise was like a ripple through the supermarket, what Pork Chop thought of as that game when you were a kid. Telephone, they called it. You'd say something to the next person, and they'd repeat it to the next, and so on and so on.

A woman came running past the front of the store with blood on her hands and shirt screaming.

"What's going on?" the cashier asked and stopped scanning items.

"Shit," Pork Chop mumbled and began pushing the items back into his shopping cart. This looked like the end of his shopping spree.

The cashier recovered and looked at Pork Chop. "Wait, I didn't ring those up yet."

"Listen to me, you need to get out of here, like now, and get home. It's not safe."

"If you don't stop, I'll call security," she said.

"In about five minutes, this place is going to go to Hell." Pork Chop put everything back in the cart and pushed it just as someone else began to scream. "Four minutes," he said and left.

The parking lot was chaotic, with people in panic.

Louise and her daughter were finishing packing the car, fear in their eyes, when he showed up. The three began grabbing items and shoving them into the car as quickly as they could.

Pork Chop turned to see a man approaching slowly from the front of the car, but they were almost done packing it. He figured he'd deal with this guy once the trunk was closed and they were ready to move.

Something odd about the man made Pork Chop turn, just in time for the man to lunge at him as if drunk and snap his teeth down on Pork Chop's jacket. "Into the car," Pork Chop yelled and kicked the man in the stomach. Instead of doubling over in pain, the man tried to grab him by the throat. Pork Chop used the man's momentum as he came on and hip-tossed him to the ground, silently thanking his mother for those karate lessons as a kid.

Pork Chop climbed into the mini-van, started it, and pulled out of the space just as the front windows of the store shattered and dozens of people exited, either through the doors or through shards of glass.

Pork Chop put the car in drive and decided he'd run over anyone that got in between them and the exit to the parking lot.

"Go find nails and a hammer in the garage," Grady said to his son and smiled, even though he felt like crying. The four sheets of plywood they'd found in the garage—warped and thin—wouldn't be of much use unless they found some nails.

While his son went to find those items, Grady decided to ask Camille about the neighbors. Maybe someone wasn't home and they could raid the house for supplies and more material to fortify this place.

"Camille?" he said, almost in a whisper. She wasn't in the living room or the kitchen. She was probably in her bedroom getting dressed. *Maybe even taking a shower if I'm lucky*, he thought. If he walked in on her, it would be an accident. He needed to talk to her right away, they were all stressed, it was an honest mistake.

She was mad as Hell right now, but Grady decided to use that to his advantage. He'd agree with whatever she said to make nice with her, go along with her in any decision making, and eventually, he'd bang her. He wondered how her brown thighs were going to look wrapped around his head. He wanted to taste that dark berry and felt his dick get hard just thinking about her.

He stood at the closed bedroom door and hesitated. What if he got lucky, she wanted him, and he was balls-deep in this momma and Drew walked in?

"Chance you gotta take," he whispered.

Grady figured this shit—whatever it was going on—would be squashed by the police soon enough and they'd be on their merry way to Orlando. He only had a small window of opportunity to sleep with Camille, and with Louise and Pork Chop gone, he decided it was game on.

He put his hand on the knob and turned it slowly. It clicked, and he pushed the door open, eyes seeking his target.

Camille was there, standing at her dresser, fully clothed, and holding a small handgun. When she saw Grady, she screamed and lifted the gun.

He fell to the ground, slamming a shoulder into the wall in the hallway.

Before he could compose himself, she was kneeling over him, gun pressed to his forehead.

"Holy shit, Camille," was all he could say.

She stared angrily down at him, the gun still against his flesh.

"I just came to ask you something," he finally said.

"Speak," she said but didn't budge.

"I was, uh, wondering if there was any more wood to barricade the windows."

Camille stared into his eyes, and Grady could almost feel the hatred, anger, and pain emanating from them. *She's a tough bitch,* he thought.

Finally, she stood and ignored him when he put his hand up for some help. "I already told you to go next door and take whatever you need."

"Dad," Drew yelled from the kitchen. "Hurry!"

4

At first, Grady didn't understand what Drew was excited about, but he was glad that Camille was no longer pointing a gun in his face.

There were three people walking slowly down the sidewalk on the other side of the street. The old man across the street who'd been watering his lawn before dark was now sitting in a rocking chair on his front stoop reading the paper.

"What?" Grady asked his son, throwing his arms up. "We don't have time for games."

"No games," Drew said angrily. "Those three people just finished eating somebody down the street, and now they're coming this way."

"Eating?" Camille asked. They stood on the front lawn and watched in terror and awe as the three shambling corpses—because the way they moved and looked, Grady knew they were dead—all turned as one and headed toward the old man across the street.

"We need to warn him," Camille said and stepped forward.

Grady put his arm out and stopped her (and noticed with

satisfaction that his hand brushed against her large left breast). "Wait, don't draw attention. They didn't see us."

"Are you insane?" Camille asked. "I'm not going to stand here while my neighbor gets bitten."

"What's his name?" Grady asked her.

"What?" she finally said, but he could see that he'd shaken her. In the movies, people go rushing headlong into danger to save the old man, who used to give them candy as a teenager, or save the nice nun or priest that took them off the mean streets. This was real life, with real consequences. Grady wasn't going to be killed for some old man no one even bothered with until right now.

"Why does that even matter?" Camille said and pushed his hand away. She leaned into him and smiled, but it wasn't friendly. "You need to stay ten feet away from me at all times, understand?"

Grady felt the gun pressed against his bulge and nodded dumbly.

"Are we going to do something?" Drew asked frantically.

"Yes, of course," Grady said but didn't know what that something was going to be. Already the three undead were on the old man's lawn, lumbering toward him, unaware in his rocking chair.

Two blocks from home Pork Chop had to pull over. The side roads they'd been driving on were empty until trying to cross Elm and Palm Streets. A three-car pileup and bodies littering the asphalt weren't the only problems: at least six undead, covered in blood, were in the intersection.

"Can't we go around them?" Louise asked.

"Shit." Pork Chop put the mini-van in reverse and began backing up. "We can cut down another street and get around the accident."

A police car, lights flashing but no siren, came out of nowhere and slammed into the side of the mini-van, lunging them five feet to their right and tossing them around the interior.

Pork Chop didn't black out, even though his face had smashed against the steering wheel. When he touched his face, he felt blood and figured his nose was broken.

Louise was slumped on the dashboard, and Isabella was on the floor.

Pork Chop touched Louise on the shoulder, fearing she was critically injured. What would he do if she were dead? If they were both dead? What if they came back as zombies?

"Are you alright?"

Pork Chop turned, startled, and looked into the face of a cop standing next to the driver's window. He looked clean-cut, fresh out of the Police Academy, with red hair and freckles. "Are you an asshole?" he said.

The cop frowned and put a hand on his holster. "Excuse me?"

Pork Chop was pissed. He knew he needed to shut up right now, but he didn't care. The rules had changed, right? "Don't you look where you're driving? Where did you even come from?"

The cop took a step back. "The side alley. I'm sorry, I was responding to an officer down. Is everyone alright?"

"I don't know." Pork Chop slowly lifted Louise's head, and she coughed. "I'm not sure about the girl."

The cop ran around to the passenger side and opened the sliding door to the mini-van, checking Isabella for a pulse. "She's alive."

"We need to get out of here." Pork Chop looked out the cracked front window and saw three zombies approaching. "We need to go now, buddy. They're coming."

"Who's coming?"

"The fucking zombies." Pork Chop turned the car key but the engine stuttered. "Fuck."

"My squad car is smoking," the cop said. "She's awake."

"Great, see if she can walk." Pork Chop shook Louise. At this point, the women were either going to move or they'd be eaten. It was as simple as that.

Pork Chop got his door open despite the damage and ran around, opening Louise's door. He helped her out of the mini-van. She was still dazed, but she was standing and nodded when he asked if she was alright.

Isabella was holding onto the cop, but she was also able to walk, which was another good sign.

"I need to get to my squad car and radio this in."

"We need to get off the street before more come our way," Pork Chop said. "I live a couple blocks away from here."

The closest undead was now only six feet away, arms extended and a mix of blood and spit dripping from its mouth.

"Shoot it," Isabella said to the cop.

Instead, he pulled his gun and pointed it. "Stop, or I will shoot."

"Are you kidding me?" Pork Chop asked. "That thing is going to bite you."

The zombie, probably a male but hard to determine under the blood, didn't stop.

"Last chance," the cop said. "I've never shot anyone before."

"Then give me the fucking gun," Pork Chop said. "Because I'll clear this street of these motherfuckers."

"Profanity isn't helping, sir. Especially in front of your daughter."

Pork Chop had to laugh, despite the predicament they were in. "Daughter? Seriously? I'm a black man, in case you hadn't noticed, Red. You don't get any whiter than her."

"Hey," Isabella said but smiled. "I could be your daughter."

"Not going to happen, little lady." Pork Chop could not believe they were having this conversation. "Either shoot it or give me the gun."

"Last chance to stop," the cop said. When the zombie was only scant inches away, he fired, hitting it in the neck. It kept coming.

"Shoot it in the fucking head," Pork Chop yelled.

The cop took a step back and fired, blowing a hole in the top of its head. It fell to the ground. "Holy shit, I just killed someone."

"He was already dead. We need to move." Pork Chop saw a stream of zombies coming from all directions.

"Let me get the shotgun from the squad car and call this in."

"Are you crazy? We need to move," Louise said groggily.

"She's right." Pork Chop took her by the hand. "I know a shortcut home, but we need to scale a fence. Come on." He pulled Louise with him across the street, hoping she'd wake up enough to keep pace. He didn't want to lose her, but she wasn't going to get him killed.

Right before ducking into the alley, he turned back and was pissed. "Let's go!" he shouted.

The cop and Isabella were standing at the squad car. He had his radio and handed her the gun.

Isabella pointed and shot a nearby zombie in the head, dropping it.

"Damn, your girl can shoot," Pork Chop said. He watched in awe as she hit three more zombies in quick succession, all kill-shots. "Where'd she learn to shoot like that?"

"Not from me and definitely not from her father." Louise pulled away from Pork Chop. "Isabella, come on."

The cop dropped the radio, pulled the shotgun, and joined Isabella in clearing a path through the creatures.

Pork Chop wished he had a gun. All he could do was stand and watch with Louise.

Suddenly the cop and Isabella were surrounded by a score of undead, and three appeared in the mouth of the alley, homing in on Pork Chop and Louise.

"We need to move."

Louise shook her head. "I won't leave without my daughter."

"Then you'll both die." Pork Chop grabbed her by the arm and pulled her away.

5

Camille ran across the street, gun drawn.

"Wait," Grady yelled. He didn't know why. *Better her than me,* he thought. There was no way he was going to save some random old man from getting killed and maybe get himself killed instead.

At the sound of his voice, the zombies turned toward him.

"Shit," Grady muttered.

Camille, running full steam, nearly crashed into the first one when it stopped. She pointed the gun and pulled the trigger, shooting it right between the eyes.

It was over quickly as she dispatched each zombie in turn with a headshot.

"Holy shit," Drew said excitedly. "She just blew their heads off like it was nothing. I have never seen anything like that. I wish I had my phone out, that so would have been on YouTube."

"Shut up," Grady said. He turned and went back into the house. Not only did Camille own a gun, but she knew how to use it. That was pretty scary.

He needed a drink, but the kitchen cabinets were devoid of alcohol, as well as the refrigerator. *Who doesn't keep a bottle of something in the house for guests?*

Grady decided he needed to get away from this crazy bitch— shit, all these crazy bitches—as soon as possible.

"Mister Higgins, have a seat right there," he heard Camille say from the living room.

"Great, now we get to babysit an old man. Who gets first diaper change?"

"Did you say something?" Camille said from the doorway. Grady noticed she was still holding the gun.

"Just talking to myself." Grady sat down at the kitchen table. "Got any alcohol?"

"For cuts?" she asked, but he could see by her expression she knew exactly what he meant. *Just another smart-ass bitch.*

"To drink and get drunk."

"Not in my house. Pork Chop . . . he doesn't drink anymore." Camille glanced back into the living room. "We have a new guest in *my* house. I suggest you play nice. I also suggest you help Drew board up the house. Those gunshots can be heard for a mile, and if there were any more in the area, they're coming."

"I guess I'll go across the street and see if he has anything we can use," Grady said. "They should be back with a shit-load of food any minute."

"They should've been back already." Camille crossed her arms. "Anytime you're ready to do something other than stare at me would be great."

Grady put up his hands and smiled, but she didn't return it. "Whatever," he mumbled and left the house. The streetlights were on, and he could see flashes of light in the distance and smell a fire somewhere nearby.

"Dad, where are you going? I need your help," Drew said from the side of the house.

"I'm going to get more wood and a hammer."

Drew held up a hammer and a coffee can that rattled with nails. "I also found wood next door. The guy had an unfinished Florida room, so I yanked plywood off the wall. Come hold this for me."

Grady stood in the middle of the street and looked both ways. It was empty, but he had a sinking feeling it wouldn't be for long. "Where are the neighbors?"

Drew shrugged. "The couple over there ran out just now and took off in their car. I saw about ten cars speeding away, too."

Grady looked at the house Drew had pointed to. He wondered what they left behind. "I'll be right back."

"Dad," Drew said, but Grady ignored him. Drew and his sister were always whining about something, always complaining when they didn't get their way. Just like their mother.

He walked up to the front door of the house and peeked in the front bay window before knocking, even though he felt stupid doing it. *Better safe than sorry*, he thought. He didn't need left-behind grandma with a shotgun killing him. Grady tried the door, not surprised it was locked.

Drew watched him from across the street. "Keep working! This isn't break time." He smiled when Drew threw his arms up in clear frustration and went back to nailing boards over the windows. "That kid could use the exercise. All he does is play video games and sleep."

Grady went around to the back of the house since they had no fence. The back was screened in, and he simply poked his hand through the screen and unlocked the door. A picnic table, some benches and chairs, and a dirty grill stood before him. Nothing of value. The sliding glass doors were also locked, but he didn't think it would be a problem.

One of the benches made an excellent projectile, and he laughed at the noise and the chaos as he slammed it into the glass and it shattered. "That was fun," he said. If he'd known it was going to be that cool and reckless, he would've done it years ago, before he got bogged down in his bullshit job and wife and ungrateful kids.

He wiped glass shards off his hands and arms, wincing at a large spike he pulled off his wrist. He was bleeding, but it wasn't that bad. Inside, in the kitchen, he washed his hands and dried them with a paper towel.

"Where to begin?" He decided to see what was for dinner since Pork Chop and Louise weren't back and he'd not finished his crappy diner food. He hoped Pork Chop was a better cook at home, or maybe sexy Camille would whip something up.

He found Swiss cheese and ham in the refrigerator, bread on the counter, and made himself two sandwiches. There were also three Miller Lites, so he popped the top off one and sat down at the table and enjoyed his meal in silence for once. No bitching wife, complaining about unpaid bills, no kids either ignoring him or asking for money.

"Maybe I'll just live here," he thought. "Why go back over there with all the bullshit?"

He left the crumbs on the table with his empty beer can, grabbed another cold one, and decided to explore his new home.

Isabella ran out of ammo and began kicking at the undead surrounding the squad car. She and the cop—his name was Jarrod Deaufrain—were trapped, and for now they could only dance on the roof of the car and step on fingers as the zombies attacked. One false move and they'd grab hold of her ankle and drag her down.

"What now?" she finally asked, out of breath from excitement and constantly moving.

"I don't know. Maybe this wasn't a great idea to get up here," he said.

"You think?" Isabella kicked a taller zombie right in the face and watched with satisfaction as teeth scattered. "This is the part where the cop saves the defenseless little girl."

"Defenseless? Heck, you shoot better than I do. You didn't miss one headshot."

"Luck." Isabella looked around. "Mom and that dude left us for dead."

"They probably went for help. There are about fifty zombies between us and them. No way they'd be able to fight through, especially without weapons."

"Still, for once I'd like mom to fight for me."

"Huh?" he said, stomping on hands.

"Nothing. This is my plan: I'm going to jump on the hood and climb onto the mini-van and take my chances on the other side. There's only a few of them on that side of the street."

"That's suicide."

"So is tiring on this roof and getting eaten. Stay here if you want."

"I'll do it." Jarrod smiled at her. "This is the part where the cop saves the girl, remember? I'll draw them away from the car, and you head down that alley and catch up with your mom."

"What about you?"

"What about me? I'll be fine. These things are slow, and I know my way around this city."

Isabella nodded. "Be careful. You know where I'll be, right?" She blushed. "For when the rescue parties are dispatched, make sure they find us."

"I know the area well." He shook her hand quickly. "Good luck, Isabella."

Jarrod jumped onto the hood and sprang up onto the crushed side of the mini-van and onto its roof. "Over here, you dumb idiots." He kicked his foot on the roof for emphasis before sliding over the side.

Isabella watched as he shoved and punched his way clear, running thirty feet up the street and shouting as he moved. The horde moved almost as one in his direction, enthralled by him.

"Run, Isabella, run!"

There were only a few in her immediate area, but she easily got away from them as she leaped off the car and sprinted into the alley. She honestly hoped Jarrod would be alright.

6

Pork Chop and Louise circled, coming back two blocks up the street. The cop and Isabella were on top of the police car, shooting at the horde around them.

"My baby," Louise yelled before Pork Chop grabbed her by the arm and dragged her back against the nearest building and out of sight.

"Are you crazy? You'll get us all killed." He looked around to make sure they weren't in any immediate danger. "We need to get back to my house and safety. I have a gun, and I'll come back and get her. I swear."

"I'm not leaving without my daughter."

Pork Chop wanted to scream, punch the brick wall in frustration, and shake this woman full of common sense.

"You told me you had no children?" she asked suddenly.

"That's right."

"Then you can't imagine what I'm going through right now, can you? That's my daughter on that car, surrounded by death. As a parent, I can't walk away from her and leave her to die. I'd rather join her than abandon her."

"Fine." Pork Chop took Louise by the hand and started pulling her away.

"Aren't you listening to me?"

He stopped. "Yes, sorry. But in order to save her we need weapons. We're in a business section right now, but the next block there are residential houses. There's also a known drug house."

"Drugs? I don't understand."

"Where there are drugs, there's usually guns. If we can get inside and get some weapons, we'll have a better chance."

"Do you think some drug dealers are going to let us have some guns?"

Pork Chop smiled. "We can always ask, right?" He didn't want to mention that the shooting had stopped around the corner. They'd run out of ammo.

Pork Chop hoped they hadn't run out of time.

"Let me do the talking," he said.

Camille offered Drew a tall glass of lemonade and a smile.

"Thank you, ma'am."

She looked around. "Where's your father?"

Drew looked away and sipped his drink.

"Please don't tell me you did the entire house by yourself."

"He was going to the houses to get supplies. He'll be back."

Camille didn't know if that was a good or bad thing. "Did he go next door?"

"No." Drew pointed at the house his dad had gone into. "I know he went around back at that one, but that's the only time I saw him."

"Now that we're secure, we can go house to house ourselves while we're waiting for Pork Chop and your mom. Want to go with me?"

"Sure. I'll bring the hammer."

"We're looking for food, water, first aid kits, toilet paper, weapons, and flashlights."

"I thought they were going to get all that at the store," Drew said.

Camille didn't want to alarm him, so she smiled. "You can never have enough toilet paper." *Besides, they've been gone way too long.* "We just need to figure out how to get into the house."

Drew smiled. "Leave that to me."

Camille followed him to the neighbor's front door, where he

pulled out his wallet. "I come prepared." A thick credit card was pulled, and he went to work. Within seconds she heard a click, and Drew pushed the door open and stepped back.

"I don't want to know where you picked up that particular skill," she said.

"Yeah, better I keep that to myself. And, uh, can we keep this between us? My dad would freak if he knew some of the shit I could do."

"Not a problem." Camille wanted to add what an asshole his dad was but decided to let it go. Maybe Grady had chickened out and left, but more than likely he was somewhere close by, sniffing dirty panties in a laundry room.

"Nice place," Drew said. "Look at the big TV."

"We don't need that. I'm sure the power will be out soon enough. We should also look for candles and matches."

"I'll start in the kitchen," Drew said. "I'm getting hungry."

"The Topper's are away for the week but live here full-time. On the other side of my house are three winter homes in a row. There's going to be nothing in those."

"I found Fruit Loops."

"Find something to carry stuff in. We should've come prepared. Didn't think of that," she said.

"Next house we'll be ready. I found some Publix shopping bags."

At the mention of Publix, Camille started to cry, knowing her husband was heading a few blocks away to get them supplies at Publix. Would he ever return? She didn't know, and the thought of losing him was tearing her up inside.

"Are you alright?" Drew asked, and she could see how uncomfortable he was.

She wiped her eyes and smiled. "Me? I'm fine. Someone cutting onions?"

Drew laughed and went back to looking. "How about knives?" he asked, pulling a large one from the blade rack on the counter.

"Take them all." Camille opened each drawer and tried to think what items they could use. There were loose batteries, and she had no idea if they even worked but shoved them in her pockets as well as a new roll of Scotch tape. Why? She had no idea. "At this point, we take random stuff."

"Yeah, I agree. No telling what we really need or when we'll be able to come back once we barricade ourselves in the house, right?"

"Right." Camille found a flashlight and tried it, but it was dead. She shoved it into a grocery bag. "The next house we'll hit will be someone that lives here all year. This isn't worth it."

"What if they're home?"

"We'll see if they want to join us." Camille found more knives in the utensil drawer. "Maybe they have more supplies, something we don't have."

"That would be cool. Maybe they have a hot daughter."

Camille laughed. She was starting to like Drew. "The Joneses have a hot daughter, about your age. She got in trouble for being a stripper and a nymphomaniac."

Drew lit up. "What house does she live in?"

"The one in your dreams."

Isabella had done some bad things in her short life. She'd had sex, smoked cigarettes and pot, shoplifted, set fire to an empty building, and stolen money from her parents. All in the last eighteen months.

She hated Louise and Grady—she decided to never call them mom and dad again—and wanted to escape from their poisoning. She knew about the affair but also knew what mom didn't know—that he'd done it more than once and with more than one other woman. Isabella had watched him and June, Dean's mom, groping one another in her garage.

That's when she decided that Dean would be her first. He didn't mean anything long-term to her, but she thought it amusing and ironic that his mom and her dad were doing it, so why shouldn't they? What would Grady ever do if he found out his darling little daughter was having sex? What could he do?

Isabella wished Dean were here with her now if only to share in the craziness. He loved to party, shoot things—he took her out to the dumps and taught her how to shoot beer cans and snakes— and he always lived recklessly. Dean knew his mother was a cheating whore (his words) and his dad was an idiot.

"Fuck that noise," she said quietly and shook her head. "Back to the fucked up present."

She had no idea where she was. The backyard she was hiding

in had only one exit through the gate, which she locked when she entered. The six-foot stockade fence blocked off the neighboring houses, and the spot she was squatting in offered her a view of the gate and the back door to the house itself.

Isabella didn't know if the people were home, but she didn't want to be caught here. This didn't look like the nicest neighborhood and adding the zombies probably didn't help, either.

A tapping on the fence toward the gate almost made her scream. She looked around for a weapon, but there wasn't anything.

Isabella always thought it was stupid in horror movies when the weakling chicks cried like bitches and covered their mouths to stifle a scream. How unrealistic.

Isabella covered her mouth, shoving her fingers into her mouth because she wanted to explode with a scream to make those actresses envious.

The house looked like every other house on the block: unkempt lawn, rusting chain-link fence, weeds growing through the warped wooden slats of the porch, and tattered blinds barely glimpsed through greasy windows. The porch light was off, either because it was simply off or because it was burnt out.

Pork Chop had no idea how to handle this, but he needed to be strong in front of Louise. Any show of weakness, and he'd be a dead man.

"Are you sure about this? Maybe she got away already. Maybe more cops showed up and she's back at the house," Louise said hopefully.

"We've already wasted way too much time. It's time to step up and save some lives." He felt no more confident as he strolled up to the gate and unhooked it. He knew they were watching him, either through the shaded windows or with the small video camera perched next to the damaged satellite dish on the roof. In the dark he could just make out the red light.

"Stay here." Pork Chop put his hands up and took a step forward.

The front door opened a crack. "What?"

"We need help."

A young kid, white with a Marlins baseball cap on, stepped onto the porch with both hands hidden behind his back. "What you need, blood?" he asked and grinned. Through the light inside spilling behind him, it was hard to tell much more. Pork Chop hoped his eyes adjusted.

"We—I'm wondering if you've any idea what's going on out here?"

"Cops?" The kid (Pork Chop guessed he was no more than fifteen) pulled two small-caliber guns out and pointed them at Pork Chop. "You the fucking cops, blood?"

"Why would I be a cop and say we need help?" This wasn't going as planned but better than he expected. "Are you watching the news?"

"The news? What the fuck you talkin' about, bitch? You got two seconds to step off my property before I blast, you get it?" For emphasis, he waved both guns.

Pork Chop stayed where he was, hands still raised. "We need weapons."

The kid laughed. "So?"

Pork Chop tried to remain calm. He didn't want to get shot and didn't want to walk away empty-handed, knowing what a stupid idea this was. Isabella was probably already dead, and any weapon they procured would be used to kill her. He glanced back at Louise on the street.

"I'll count to three, and then I'll shoot your black ass," the kid said.

"Fine." Pork Chop started backing away.

"Are you serious? We need a gun," Louise said and rushed to the gate.

"One . . . two . . . "

Pork Chop turned and grabbed Louise, holding her back.

"Hey, I'll trade you that old white bitch of yours for a gun."

Louise pulled away from Pork Chop. "Really?"

"Are you nuts?" Pork Chop whispered.

The kid laughed. "Yeah, her old ass and five grand."

"Thank you anyway." Pork Chop pushed Louise away. "We need to get out of here."

"What the fuck is that?" The kid yelled as a fireball rose into the air less than a mile away.

"Put the news on. There's a war out here, blood."

8

"That's Syd Gossling," Camille said quietly to Drew.

They stood in the backyard, checking and rechecking the boarded-up windows. On the other side of the short wooden fence stood Syd, blood dripping from his mouth. They hadn't noticed him until his movements tripped the motion sensor lights.

"Don't move," Drew said. He held the hammer in his hands but didn't want to get close to Syd if he could help it. Maybe he wouldn't notice them and would move on.

On the patio behind the house, they could see a pile of body parts, covered in gore and blood. It was so mutilated that you couldn't tell if it was a man or a woman, but the blood trail led right to Syd, standing unmoving in the grass. An old rusting swing set was the only thing between him and them, and the rickety fence.

Camille took a step toward the house but stopped when Syd turned his head in their direction.

Drew squeezed the hammer. Could he use it to kill someone else if he had to? Was Syd even a 'someone else' at this point?

Syd opened his mouth, and a chunk of something dark and dripping fell from his mouth and onto the grass. He was looking right at them but not moving.

Camille yelped when the motion detector light went out, plunging them back into the darkness of night. There weren't many stars through the cloud cover.

Drew could feel Camille next to him but couldn't see her. "We need to get back inside."

Camille didn't respond. The only sound was Syd obviously hitting the swing set because the rusty chains started to creak.

Drew, still trying to see Syd but failing, reached out to grab Camille. "We need to go," he whispered.

A thump against the wooden fence and he almost wet himself. He spun and grabbed the silhouette that was Camille, one hand on her shoulder and the other hand grabbing her left breast. Embarrassed, he gripped her arm and led her back to the front of the house. She was quiet but let Drew lead her.

Inside, Drew closed and locked the front door and put her on the couch next to Mister Higgins.

The silk robe fit tightly around his gut, but Grady didn't mind. The bath had been magnificent: no one complaining about him taking too long, no one bitching about no more hot water, and no one trying to jump in the bathroom before he did.

He sat down on the couch and reached for the TV remote but stopped. There were noises outside in the dark on the street. He crept to the living room windows and hid behind the curtain, peeking out to the front steps.

There was someone out there, just standing out of range of the porch light. "Why did you turn that on, dumb-ass?" he whispered. He closed the heavy curtains—they were brown and heavy, and he knew he'd need to replace them with something more colorful now that he lived here—and turned off the light on the end table, plunging the room in darkness. "Better safe than sorry." He decided against shutting the porch light off. No telling how smart these things were and what might attract a bunch more.

Grady shuffled to the kitchen, turned off the overhead light, and made sure the back door was locked and bolted. Not that it mattered because the glass had been shattered and a nice breeze came right into the kitchen. Tomorrow he would get up early and go down to the Home Depot and get a new door, something sturdy.

For now, he pushed the kitchen table against the door and piled all the chairs on top. The kitchen décor was boring, little fat Italian pizza guys everywhere. He decided to redo it with something more manly. Maybe NASCAR or baseball, even though he wasn't much of a sports fan.

He was about to start redecorating but decided there was always tomorrow. He was getting tired. An early start to the day, with the sun shining, would give him fresh ideas. Grady searched the cabinet and smiled when he saw the unopened pack of Oreo cookies. He poured himself a nice, big glass of milk and took the entire package of snacks to the living room. He no longer had to share what was rightfully all his, since he paid for everything. He was the breadwinner, the alpha male who brought home the proverbial bacon.

For the first time since college, he could enjoy an entire box of cookies by himself. It was going to be a good night.

There was definitely something moving on the porch outside.

Grady ignored the thump, dipping two cookies at a time into the milk. When some splashed on the rug, he left it. He'd clean it tomorrow instead of rushing to the kitchen, finding the rags and spray cleaner, and getting it up before Louise saw it.

Something crashed against the front door, and he jumped in his seat. Grady tiptoed to the front window and looked out. There was someone—some*thing*—out there, pressed against the door. Dirtying the stoop and probably getting bloody handprints on the door.

Grady went back into the kitchen and looked for a weapon, something quiet he could use to scare the thing away. He didn't see much of use.

He went to the garage. "Pay-dirt," he mumbled. There were tools hanging on three walls, with a big red Sears Craftsman tool set to one side. A Harley motorcycle, in many parts, was strewn across the floor. "What to use?" he asked himself. He put a hand on one of the parts to the bike but decided not to use it. He'd always wanted a motorcycle. Maybe with all his free time he could rebuild this one and ride. How cool would that be, wind whipping his hair back, out on the open road? He needed a few more things tomorrow: a black leather jacket, a helmet (he didn't see one in the garage), and a pair of bitchin' black leather fingerless gloves. Oh, and big black boots.

Grady stood there, looking around, and realized he'd forgotten why he'd come in here in the first place. It was cold in the garage. He tightened his robe. His feet were cold. He needed to find a good pair of slippers as well. Grady's new life was going to be amazing, but first he needed some supplies. A new wardrobe to compliment his new Hell's Angels lifestyle would be first.

Weapon forgotten, he went back to the living room and finished off the box of cookies before retiring to the bedroom. He decided to sleep in the nude since Louise always hated when he did that, and with kids in the house, it was frowned upon.

The banging at the front door had ceased.

9

One minute it was silent, and the next her ears were popping with the sound of gunfire and the flash on the other side of the gate.

"Let me in," she heard a familiar voice. It was the cop. It was also accompanied by two more shots fired.

Isabella jumped up and unlocked it, and Jarrod came barreling in, closing the gate behind him. He stared at her. "Are you hurt? Bitten?"

"No. You?"

"I'm fine. But I'm out of ammo. I tried to get to you, but these things are everywhere."

"What are they?"

Jarrod shrugged. "Who knows? Who cares, right? They're trying to bite us. We need to get out of town."

"My parents . . . " Isabella started to say but stopped. What about them? They'd left her for dead. This cop was here to protect her, not her mother or father. They were holed up, safe and sound, while she was being attacked. "Yes, we need to get out as soon as possible."

"I think if we can get back to a main road, I can flag down someone and we'll be fine."

"Is this just here, or is it everywhere?"

Jarrod shrugged. "I don't know. I have no radio contact with anyone, and the only people I saw were running away from those things. We need to move. I cleared them out but if they can still hear, those gunshots will bring them."

They opened the gate and burst into the street. They were surrounded, but there were only a few of them drifting aimlessly, and it looked like they hadn't been spotted yet.

Isabella felt herself blush as the cop took her hand, and they jogged across the street and between two buildings before stopping. He faced her. "It's a long way to the police station from here. Where are your parents?"

Isabella shrugged. "I don't know."

"I don't even remember if they told me the address. Darn."

Isabella smiled. "Darn? With everything going down, you say darn? How about shit? Fuck! Sonofabitch."

Jarrod turned away. "I'm not going to curse in front of a kid."

Isabella felt like she'd been slapped. "I'm fifteen."

"Exactly."

"How old are you?" she asked.

Jarrod hesitated. "I'm older than you. We need to run."

"Where are we going?"

"To the main road, I guess." Jarrod grabbed her hand again, but this time she was mad. This guy was maybe twenty-two, twenty-three tops. He was acting like he was so much more mature and older than her. Fuck that noise. She wasn't some little girl, led around by her hand like a baby. She pulled away from him, but he didn't seem to notice.

"I thought you were out of ammo," she said to him as they moved.

"I am." Jarrod held the shotgun out. "But they don't know that, and anyone stupid enough to get in our way doesn't know that."

"I think we came this way," Isabella said. "Isn't the diner around here?"

Jarrod smiled. "Yes. Maybe we can get inside and use the phone. Good thinking."

"No problem." At least she knew the diner, even though she'd only spent a few minutes inside. It was the starting point of all this shit for her. They entered the diner like a normal, dysfunctional family on vacation and left it a bigger mess, with their lives in danger. Now, they were split up and scattered in this falling neighborhood.

Isabella thought of her brother, Drew, and sighed. He could be an asshole and try to be her father at times, but she knew he loved her. In school and out, he was always watching over her. She'd complain openly to her friends and her parents, but she was glad he was there, and he'd gotten her out of a few minor scrapes in the last year or two. She hoped he was safe.

Jarrod stopped as they entered the back parking lot of the diner, eyes scanning the abandoned cars. "It's too quiet."

Isabella noticed it as well. She assumed, once they got to the diner and close to the main road, the sound of traffic would be prevalent. Instead, it was eerily silent. "What do you think?"

"I think we skirt around the diner and see what's going on out front. We'll get a better idea for our game plan." He tapped the empty shotgun. "Are you ready to move?"

"Yes." Isabella gripped the back of his uniform shirt. "Lead the way, officer."

They kept low, listening for any sounds, but there were none. Not even a bird flew overhead. At the back of the diner they paused, Jarrod glancing quickly through the screen door into the kitchen. He shook his head and shrugged when Isabella looked at him.

Around the left of the diner they moved slowly, trying not to make a sound. As they got to the side, Isabella could see the road. There were abandoned cars on it and one was smoking, but no one was around. She looked into the big bay windows of the diner and saw it was empty, the power out, and no one in sight.

As they got into the front parking lot, Jarrod held up his hand. "Do you hear that?"

She stopped to listen and heard it: a scraping noise, in the distance. It was getting louder.

"I'm going to check it out."

"Don't leave me," she blurted.

Jarrod chuckled. "I'm going to walk to the street and see what the noise is. Maybe it's the National Guard coming to save us."

"Maybe. Hurry up." She felt stupid, like a little kid.

Isabella watched as he ducked and moved around the cars in the parking lot and got to the sidewalk, looking first left and then right. She knew by the way his body stiffened and he gripped the shotgun there was something wrong.

He ran back, fear in his eyes. "We need to run."

Isabella didn't bother asking any questions, turning and heading back the way they'd come. "Fuck."

There were dozens of them entering the far end of the back parking lot.

"Into the diner," Jarrod said, and they ran back to the front of the diner, opening the glass front doors as quietly and quickly as he could.

Isabella stifled a scream when she saw the horde of walking dead coming down the street.

"We need to get back to your house," Louise said to Pork Chop.

"How? Dance our way through a wall of them? We need a weapon."

"We need to get somewhere safe. My daughter is alone, and my son is probably going crazy with worry about me."

"What about your husband?"

Louise smiled faintly. "I doubt it. He's more than likely hitting on your wife."

"Then he's more than likely on the floor, holding his privates and wondering why she kicked him in them. Camille is one tough lady. That's why I love her."

"I used to love Grady." Louise looked away, tears welling. "He used to love me."

"Well, then God might be giving you both a second chance here. But first, we need to get off the street and not be a target. I know the area pretty well, but I don't have many friends I can pop in on and ask for a gun."

Louise began to shake. Pork Chop gripped her by the shoulders and looked her square in the eyes. "Listen to me, okay? If you meltdown right now, we're both dead. You can kiss your kids goodbye, and I can kiss my wife goodbye. You don't want that, and neither do I. Please, please, I am begging you, get your stuff together and help me help us. We need to move."

He could see her face change. One moment she was a helpless girl, and the next she was a tough woman, acting her age and knowing her responsibilities. And her only focus was survival.

When Louise nodded, Pork Chop smiled at her. "It's going to be alright."

"Where do we go?"

"Let's try to get home first. I agree with that. Come on, there might be a way through some side streets." There was no clear way to get back to his house without getting back onto a main road, and he didn't want to do it if he could help it. But if they tried to cross over through people's yards and around properties, they were liable to get shot, too.

They jogged half a block before the way ahead was suddenly blocked by a group of the dead, all staggering in their direction.

"We need to find another way," Pork Chop said. He ran to the nearest house and peered over the fence. A dog began to growl and slammed into the fence on the other side. "That won't work."

10

"He's sleeping," Camille said quietly to Drew. They'd moved Mister Higgins into the guest room from the couch, more for something to do and calm their nerves than for anything else.

Camille felt lost. Drew was staring at her, waiting for a decision. But what decision?

"I guess we'll do another walk of the house and make sure the windows are locked and shades pulled. There's no movement outside. Have you ever shot a gun before?" Camille asked Drew.

He shook his head. "I'm sixteen."

Camille smiled. "I was ten when I had my first lesson on shooting. Hell, I shot two deer and numerous squirrels by the time I was sixteen."

His eyes got big. "Wow. Really?"

"Killing a deer for food is far different from shooting another person, even if they're not right," she said quietly. "I hope, if it comes to that, you can pull the trigger."

"So do I," Drew admitted. "When is my family coming back?"

Camille shrugged. "I don't know. Hopefully soon. I need my husband back, too. I'm sure it will be soon."

She knew they were all likely dead. What was she going to do with this kid now? Like Mister Higgins, he was more a liability than help. He might be able to nail some boards to the windows but not much else.

"Hopefully they'll have plenty of food," Camille said. She went in and checked on Mister Higgins, who was snoring softly in the guestroom.

Where is everyone going to sleep? Is Drew's asshole father coming back, or did he abandon his family? This is all too much, Camille thought.

She went through the pantry and the cabinets again, trying to figure out how much food she really had. The power was still working, but she didn't know for how long. They had the old rusting grill in the backyard, but the smell of meat cooking might draw the dead.

How does their smell work? They can see, Camille thought.

"Drew, can you help me?" Camille said, popping back into the living room.

He was staring out the small window in the door.

"I think someone is walking down the street. It might be my mom," Drew said.

Camille waved her hand. "Do not open the door. Wait until it gets closer."

Drew looked at her and frowned. "She looks hurt. It is my mom, not an it."

"Sorry. We can't be too careful." Camille was about to say more when he opened the door.

"No, wait," she said, rushing across the living room.

Drew was already outside and yelling for his mom.

Camille saw the thing in the street was definitely not his mother. It was female, but that's where the likeness ended.

The monster's body was naked and covered in blood, huge gashes across both breasts, and a neck wound that had likely dumped a lot of blood from it before the woman died.

"Drew, come inside," Camille yelled. She could see more movement in the dark, coming down the street.

Camille groaned as she lost Drew in the darkness.

Grady went through all of the drawers in the bedroom, imagining the woman who'd lived there being super hot and sexy. Not that her underwear drawer bore that out; the bras and panties sets were for an old woman. Everything beige. No frills, no thongs, nothing even remotely exciting.

I'll have to go door to door at some point and find a young woman's lingerie. Maybe some porn home videos, Grady thought. He'd tried in the beginning of his marriage to get Louise onboard to film themselves, but that was a hard no.

Louise hadn't spoken to him for over a week, a look of disgust every time they were near one another.

She thought he was going to try to post them on some weird pornographic site, one of the websites he liked to search. Porn sites he'd sworn he'd stopped watching once they were married.

Grady smiled. He'd never stopped. Since she'd become such a cold, rigid bitch, he'd watched them even more now.

And he knew, if she had been conned into filming, he would definitely share it with the site and have other members trade for their own wives and videos.

The search of the rest of the house was a waste of time. Whoever the male was living here, he wasn't into dirty magazines or anything exciting.

Grady groaned when he peeked into the garage and saw the train set. This guy was an idiot, playing with trains instead of himself.

Even the slow laptop in the living room had no hidden files. The internet was down so Grady couldn't spend his night surfing the web for free porn.

What did these people do for fun?

Grady was going to have fun soon enough, as soon as things settled down out there. He'd find a few women and enslave them.

This is going to be a new world, Grady thought.

A world where he could do anything he wanted. He'd amass as much cash and valuable items as he possibly could, starting tomorrow. He'd ransack every home on this block. Taking whatever he wanted.

He thought of Camille and knew she was definitely what he wanted.

She was going to be a fighter, and he smiled at the thought of breaking her.

When did you get so horny and bold? This is a new me, and I like it, Grady thought.

He'd need to search for weapons, too. He was sure most residents had guns. This was Florida, dammit.

Tonight he'd need to get some good sleep. He knew he had a long day ahead of him tomorrow.

He crawled into bed and wondered when the last time anyone had had sex in it. Probably not for a long time.

Grady closed his eyes and imagined what he would do to Camille, once he'd secured weapons and possibly some rope. Handcuffs would be nice, too.

Whatever it took to make the sexy black woman his concubine.

11

The diner was trashed, but the windows were still mostly intact. The power had gone out, and the smell of food made Isabella's stomach groan.

Jarrod led the way inside, through the smashed doors, sweeping his weapon back and forth.

Isabella could see the zombies outside, slowly shuffling toward the diner.

"We need to block the doors," Jarrod said. "Help me with these tables."

The booth tables were bolted to the floor, but there were a couple of tables used by the waitresses, including a rolling cart made of wood that looked heavy.

They rolled it to the door and dropped it onto its side, hoping it would trip the zombies or at least slow them down.

A few tables were jammed against it as well as the hostess stand and anything else heavy they could find, creating a wall they hoped would hold.

"If the zombies can climb, we're screwed," Jarrod said. He pointed at the windows. "Nothing to block them."

Isabella was shaking. She needed to keep moving, to have something to do.

She went into the kitchen and found a set of very large and sharp knives.

Jarrod came into the back and smiled, taking one of the knives from her. "I think, if we stay out of sight, they won't try to get us. I'm not sure if that's really going to happen. More of a theory."

"Well, I hope you're right." Isabella sat up on one of the counters so she had a view of the front. "They're at the windows."

"Stay low. Maybe we shouldn't talk. Do you think they can hear?"

Isabella shrugged. She had a knife in hand as if that would do much if a dozen of the monsters got inside. "I'm hungry," she whispered.

Jarrod nodded and slowly started to look around the kitchen.

Isabella watched as more and more zombies came to the front of the diner, but none of them seemed to be able to climb. They pushed against the tables blocking the door, but it was holding. For now.

"I guess I'm not going to worry about my diet," Jarrod said quietly and held up two pies: an apple and a blueberry.

"Apple," Isabella whispered and smiled.

"There are a couple more of each, so we're fine for a few days if we need to hide out here." Jarrod peeked out to the front and shook his head. "More pies and cakes in the display case, too."

Isabella wished the grill worked. She wanted a burger and fries. She couldn't remember the last time she'd eaten. She wondered where they'd left the mini-van and if the food had already been taken by other survivors, or if her mother had actually gotten back to Pork Chop's house and was worried.

She thought about her brother, too. Was he scared? Isabella wondered about her father, too. He'd been unstable lately, angry and then happy within a few minutes. When she'd quietly asked her father if he needed help, maybe he was bipolar, he'd snapped at her.

"I guess we try to get comfortable," Jarrod said. "I'll take first watch. Get some sleep. There has to be an office, and they hopefully have a couch."

Isabella nodded and went to the back of the diner, making mental notes of the food items she saw. Not much to live off of long-term, but the next week or so might not be bad.

If the zombies didn't burst in and kill them.

There was an office and, more importantly, a ratty couch.

Isabella put the knife on the floor, within easy reach, and tried to get comfortable.

It was too dark, which made no sense.

There were no windows in the office, and even with the door open, there were no lights.

She thought she heard a noise from outside. The back door was on the other side of the wall, and she had a bad feeling. She got up and walked to the door.

It was unlocked.

Isabella locked it and dragged a couple of rolling setup trays to block it, hoping it would hold or at least give her a warning if the door was somehow opened.

Jarrod came over to see what was happening, but she told him to go back to the front to keep watching for trouble.

Satisfied she'd taken care of the problem and feeling good about herself, Isabella went back to the couch and prayed silently that she'd get through the night.

"You can't do that to the dog," Louise said to Pork Chop. "That's . . . cruel."

Pork Shop shook his head. "Find somewhere to hide, to get out of sight. It's a dog-eat-dog world right now." Pork Chop smiled, despite the situation, because he'd come up with a good one-liner.

As the zombies approached, Pork Chop gripped the wooden slats on the fence. He waited until Louise was out of sight before he used all of his strength to yank on the gate door, shuffling it back and forth until he heard the cracking of the wood as it strained against the lock.

The zombies were maybe five feet from him now, and he only had a few seconds to try this before abandoning the plan and running.

Pork Chop dug his heels into the dirt and kept pulling, the wood still splitting, the zombies still coming.

The fence ripped in two, a jagged piece in his hands as he fell backward onto the ground, the top part of the fence coming with him.

Pork Chop closed his eyes when he heard the dog's growl and felt the weight of it on the board, pressed against his head.

Then the weight was gone, and Pork Chop pushed the wood away and rolled over.

Zombies were going after the dog, who snapped and barked and danced around them.

Time to run, Pork Chop thought.

He got up and sprinted in the direction he'd seen Louise heading, hoping to catch up to her.

"Here," Louise yelled as Pork Chop rounded the corner of a house and went right past her. She was hiding in the bushes, but there wasn't room for him, too.

"Time to go," Pork Chop said, and Louise came out. They began running up the street. No zombies in sight, but he knew it wouldn't be long before they ran right into them again.

"They seem to be gathering, like in a horde," Louise said. "That group is working together."

Pork Chop thought she was right. "Then we make sure we skip over the large mobs of them, I guess. This way."

He knew where he was headed right now because getting home seemed blocked at the moment. If the zombies were starting to gather together, maybe they'd move out of the area once their food supply was gone.

Pork Chop didn't want to be their next meal.

"I know where we're going, and I think I can get us there, as long as no one still living messes with us," Pork Chop said. "Follow me."

As the dog barked and kept the attention of the monsters, Pork Chop led Louise down the street, cutting across front yards and keeping an eye out for more trouble.

He'd come this way a few times over the years when he had car trouble and Camille had already left for the day. He'd planned the route out and even though he'd hardly ever had to use it, he knew it like the back of his hand.

Pork Chop remembered last year when he'd been getting thick in the middle and gone on a keto diet. He'd also begun walking to work, using this route.

Until it had rained on him halfway to work, and he'd smelled like a wet dog the rest of the day. Everyone in the diner had made fun of him, so he decided his walking would be done at night if he was off or worked the day shift.

He slipped between two fences, the neighbors having erected them at different times without them ever touching. Pork Chop always wondered which family did it first, and why the other hadn't simply butted their fence against the other. It created an alley that most people could fit through. If you knew it was there.

Louise gripped his arm just as they entered, and Pork Chop looked back to see a dozen zombies shuffling in their direction from across the street.

Pork Chop nodded and began moving faster. There was no one or nothing else in the alley, but he knew if zombies came from the front, they'd be trapped.

He got to the other end and peeked out. A few zombies down the road, but none in the path he was going.

Pork Chop stepped onto the street, making sure Louise was right behind him and started to move to the next spot where he could cross over a side street.

"Hey, what's going on already, buddy? Is that you, Pork Chop?"

Pork Chop turned to see one of the other cooks, a newer one, he couldn't remember his name, walking on the sidewalk.

There were at least ten zombies on his heels, and the man didn't know.

Pork Chop pointed and cried out but it was too late. The man was knocked down, and the zombies began to feast.

Pork Chop was already heading down the side street.

He didn't even know the man's name.

12

Drew wasn't coming back, and if he did, he'd hopefully be seen.

Camille hoped he didn't come back as a zombie, though. There was no doubt she'd put him down quickly. No hesitation. She hardly knew the kid, and if he was stupid enough to run outside when there were zombies present, so be it.

She checked on Mister Higgins again, but he was still asleep.

Camille hadn't gotten any sleep last night, pacing the living room and peeking out the windows.

There was a lot of activity outside, but it was mostly shadows and a glimpse of a dead person, covered in blood, shuffling down the sidewalk or street.

Her husband was still out there, somewhere. Safe. She felt it. Pork Chop would get focused and survive.

This family he'd taken in . . . she wasn't sure if any of them would make it. They seemed soft and weak. The husband had run off, and that was fine with her. The guy gave Camille the creeps. The kids seemed flighty, too. The wife? She might be the only one with a chance because she was with Pork Chop right now. Hopefully for her.

The daughter, too. As long as she stayed with Pork Chop, things had a chance to work out.

The power had flickered on and off all night. The TV was out, the cable down.

Camille had no idea what was happening out there, but she wasn't curious enough to step outside.

As the sun rose, she had a better idea of what was happening on her block. It wasn't good. There were zombies up and down the street, all shuffling back and forth and sometimes into each other.

They weren't on her property, but a few were on the sidewalk, and she wondered where they were all headed.

Camille needed to sleep, but she was afraid they might break in or hear her snoring and investigate. Her husband said she could wake the dead some nights. She hoped he wasn't actually right.

Mister Higgins was making noise in the other room, so she went to investigate. What if the old man had been bitten? Maybe he was turning into a zombie. Could she kill him?

Camille knew she could and she would. No questions asked.

He was sitting up on the bed and looked confused, staring blankly at her.

"Mister Higgins, would you like some coffee or something to eat?" Camille realized she didn't know his first name. They'd only been the typical waving neighbors all these years.

"Do you have decaf?"

Camille doubted it but nodded.

"Please help me to the bathroom. I can take care of the rest once I get there," Mister Higgins said.

As Camille helped the old man shuffle to the bathroom, he smiled at her. "Hell of a night, I guess. I dreamed there were monsters trying to kill us. Ain't that a hoot?"

Camille decided she'd explain everything to him once he was finished with his business. "I'll make some coffee. Maybe scramble an egg or two."

Mister Higgins nodded before closing the bathroom door.

She wondered if she should check his body for bite marks or blood.

There were actually two decaf coffee K-cups she found in the back of the cabinet, likely having come with the coffeemaker.

Camille set it up and went room to room, looking out the windows, wondering if anyone else was going to come back to the house.

She scrambled eggs and had the table set when the lights flickered on and off a couple of times. Camille worried most of the food would rot.

Mister Higgins shuffled to the kitchen and sat down, taking a sip of the coffee.

"What crazy dreams I had," he said and shook his head. He stared at Camille. "Aren't you the neighbor? You and your husband? Where's my Suzy?"

Camille smiled at the man. His wife, Suzy, had passed away several years ago.

"I'm sure the crazy dreams are nothing compared to what's really happening outside," Camille said.

The lights flickered again.

If the power goes out, we might have to leave, Camille thought. *Find food and shelter.*

She decided to start piling anything food-wise that didn't need to be cooked or stored in the fridge into a pile, and then break it down into what would be best to take with her. Maybe fill a suitcase with protein bars, cereal boxes, and canned veggies and soup in case they found something to cook it on.

Camille needed to keep busy, because thinking about where her husband was, if he was still alive, and if she'd survive . . . it was all too stressful.

Mister Higgins downed his coffee and smacked his lips, holding up the empty cup. "I usually drink three or four cups each morning. Be a dear and fetch me another."

Camille was about to explain they had to ration everything when something slammed against the front door.

Grady hadn't had a good night's sleep like that in years. He scrubbed his face and decided to grow his beard out, staring at his face in the bathroom mirror.

Maybe an earring would look cool, too. He wondered if a gold tooth would be going too far.

He got dressed and cracked open the back door. It was quiet. No gunshots, no zombies making noise, no birds singing. It was as if the world had gone silent.

Grady took his time going to the next yard over, hopping the fence and peeking in the back windows. There was no one home as far as he could tell. He moved his hand to knock but thought better of it. In this quiet, that knock might carry for blocks. Miles, maybe.

He tried the back door and the windows but everything was locked.

I'll search the block for an open window before starting over again and breaking in, Grady thought. He had all day. Hell, he had the rest of his life. He was a free man. The king of this new world.

Five houses down, the side door to the garage was unlocked. He went inside. There was no car in the garage, which he took for a good sign. Maybe they weren't home.

The door into the house was locked, but he kicked it in, feeling great like he hadn't felt in years. Ever since he'd gotten married and had kids.

"Hello? Police," Grady yelled. "I'm here to help."

He counted to ten but didn't hear movement. The garage led into the kitchen. He opened the fridge and found a dozen eggs, a loaf of bread and milk, as well as bacon and sausage.

Grady made himself a huge breakfast after checking out the rest of the house.

"Jackpot," he said with a laugh when he saw the many pictures on the walls and in the master bedroom: two women lived here. Together. A couple.

They each had their own underwear drawer, and he tossed them all on the bed. One of the women looked to be smaller than the other. She was Asian while her partner was maybe Latina. A bit thicker with more hips.

Grady made two piles of their bras and panties and smiled.

He checked the laundry basket, hoping to find some dirty undies, but it looked like they'd recently done all of the laundry and put it all away.

There were no sex toys like he always imagined lesbians had on hand like he'd seen on so many porn videos.

He ate breakfast and filled a box with items he might need, placing the box inside the garage.

Grady kept away from the house his family was staying at, not wanting to see them. He was done with that life.

For the next several hours, he went house to house in a three-block radius, hiding from roaming hordes of zombies and the occasional living person.

All told, he got into six houses and filled several boxes with food and items to pass the time, like a few books and some hand-held video gaming systems.

He also found three Glock hand cannons and four hunting rifles in one house. He took the weapons with him and put them in his new home.

Carrying a Glock in hand, Grady strode down the street, feeling like a badass. Like he was in charge.

He'd heard an occasional gunshot, but it was in the distance. The zombies seemed to be getting thicker, though, and he wondered if they'd eventually move on. Leaving these streets to Grady.

He'd make sure the concubines he enslaved knew how to build fences and traps. They'd section off three blocks and make sure no one could get inside the compound.

Grady was back in his new home making cheeseburgers on the stove when he glanced out the back window and saw the woman, bleeding, fall over the fence.

13

They'd survived the night without any problems, and Jarrod felt confident they could keep going as long as it took to clean up this mess.

Zombies were still in the parking lot and out back of the diner, but not as many as when they'd first arrived yesterday.

Isabella cut a cherry pie in half, and they ate it while sitting at the counter, watching the world outside the windows.

"Do you think we'll get out of here?" Isabella asked.

"And go where?"

Isabella shrugged. "I dunno. My parents are in a house somewhere nearby."

"Do you know which house, or how to get there?" Jarrod asked. "I live across town in an apartment. It wasn't that nice even before the zombies."

"No. I was only there for a few minutes. Everything is so jumbled. Maybe we wait here. This was the last place my family was all together. Maybe they'll come back for me?" Isabella sighed and took another bite. "At least we have some food."

Jarrod worried they'd need to eat as much of it as possible before it went bad. The lights had flickered on and off several times overnight before finally giving out.

Isabella finished her pie and walked the diner, looking out the windows.

"Make sure they don't see you, or we're in trouble," Jarrod said.

"I know," Isabella snapped.

Jarrod had to smile at her attitude. He wondered if many fifteen-year-olds would still be this feisty.

Isabella stopped and put her face against the glass.

Jarrod was about to yell at her to move back, but she put up a hand.

"Drew is out there. I can see him, lying under a car," Isabella said and smiled. "He's still alive."

Jarrod rushed to the window and saw the boy. He waved at Drew, but the kid wasn't looking in their direction. He was watching a new group of zombies heading toward the diner.

"We need to get him to go to the back door," Jarrod said.

Isabella went back to the counter and grabbed one of the placemats, turning it over and scribbling on it with some of the remaining cherry pie.

She stuck it against the window where she'd been and Jarrod smiled.

It said, roughly, BACK DOOR.

Drew finally glanced over at them and read the sign, nodding. He slid out from under the car and ran.

Jarrod and Isabella rushed to the back door and opened it, letting Drew in.

There were several zombies that saw this and headed toward them now.

Isabella and Drew hugged while Jarrod got the door locked and slid everything back against it.

"What happened to you?" Drew asked.

Isabella pointed at Jarrod. "He saved me. We've been hiding here since last night. You?"

"I did something stupid. I left the house and then got lost. I hid under cars all night. Almost got bit a few times, too. A lot of zombies kept bumping into a car I was under and nearly knocked it over."

Jarrod sighed. "Son, I'd hate to do this, but we need to be careful. Mind if we check you for bites? That's what seems to turn people into these monsters."

Drew nodded and rolled up his sleeves and pant legs. He hadn't been bitten.

"Can you find your way to the house?" Isabella asked.

Drew groaned. "No. I already told you. I got lost. I know it's close, but I have no idea where it is."

"For now we stay here. Your parents might try to get back to the diner, and they'll join us," Jarrod said. He hoped. Now he had two teenagers to protect.

"Dad is gone," Drew said.

"Killed?"

Drew shook his head. "No. He ran off. To another house. On his own. Instead of helping any of us."

Isabella shook her head. "He is such a jerk."

"He always was and always will be," Drew said. "I'm hungry."

"There's apple pie." Jarrod got Drew a fork and a pie.

Drew took a bite and smiled. "Any ice cream? Before it all melts?"

Isabella laughed and took two steps toward the kitchen when she stopped.

It sounded like someone or something was trying to get inside, through the back door.

She wanted to ask Pork Chop where he was taking her but didn't want to stop and have a conversation while there were so many zombies wandering the area.

Zombies? This can't be real, Louise thought.

It was morning, and they'd slept huddled together in a fenced-in backyard, inside a shed that smelled of gasoline, oil, and grass cuttings.

Pork Chop had held up two fingers. "Two blocks to go, but we can't keep doing it in the dark. We'll walk right into one of them, especially since the street lights are out now."

It made sense, although Louise was willing to chance it if they found a secure place to hide for a while. How long was a while, though? She needed to see her kids again.

Maybe even Grady, Louise thought.

They moved slowly, methodically, keeping as much distance between them and the zombies as possible.

Louise stayed a step behind Pork Chop and let him lead the way since he knew where he was going. She wanted to get back to his house but knew there were too many zombies in that direction.

Maybe if we'd stayed in the shed and waited a few hours, they might walk off, she thought but knew it wasn't safe. If one of them made a noise or a wandering zombie saw them, they were trapped.

Better to find a safe haven and see how all of this played out.

Pork Chop got to the top of the next block and looked around. Louise thought he looked unsure where to go next.

She touched his shoulder lightly and stared, her eyes asking what he wanted to do.

Pork Chop pointed ahead. "I don't see a zombie for a few blocks, even on the main road. We might be able to make it across, follow the ditch past the school, and get into the woods. I doubt there are many zombies on the other side."

"We can't leave our families," Louise said.

Pork Chop nodded. "No. We need to keep the route in mind for *when* we hook up with them, though. It might be our only chance. This city has millions of residents, plus tourists, plus people driving through. Millions. That's a lot of zombies to fight through for freedom."

Louise sighed. "What's your other plan?"

"The diner. I have a key to the doors. We can go inside and hide. Find food and water," Pork Chop said. "If the power is still working, maybe make a cup of coffee. Their apple pie is delicious, too."

"Lead the way." Louise hoped her family might be there, too. It would make sense since it was the only place they really knew here except Pork Chop's home.

They skirted across a few lawns, and Louise tried to ignore all of the blood and body parts littering the grass.

No wonder I keep seeing so many without arms or legs, they seem to attack in a frenzy and bite off limbs until the person is dead, she thought.

At the other end of the block was a massive amount of zombies, maybe even a hundred, but when Pork Chop stopped and put up his hand, none of them initially noticed them.

Until Pork Chop and Louise started walking, slowly, across the street, and Louise, watching the zombies, tripped over something metallic.

The clang of it sent a shiver up her spine, and she held her breath.

None of the zombies looked their way for at least five seconds.

Louise took two more steps before several zombies turned in their direction.

"Now we run," Pork Chop said.

14

At first, Camille hoped it was Pork Chop pounding on the door to let him in. She almost opened it but looked first.

A score of zombies were at the front door, and more were moving through the yard.

It's like a herd, Camille thought. Like you see on the wildlife shows on TV. They were all moving in the same direction, looking for the next victim.

They were banging against it, bodies being pushed against the door. The windows. The house itself.

"We need to leave," Mister Higgins said. "Step aside, woman."

Camille shook her head and blocked the old man, stumbling to the door. "No. They'll kill us."

"Not if we kill them first." Mister Higgins held two butter knives in his hands.

Camille tried to take the knives from him, but even for his age, he was strong.

Mister Higgins held onto the butter knives and looked into her eyes.

"Let me do this. I have nothing left to live for. I want to go out a hero," he said to her, eyes pleading.

There was a crash from the kitchen. It sounded like the back door was being splintered and broken down. They'd be inside in seconds.

"There are two things I've never done in my long life," Mister Higgins said. He suddenly leaned forward and kissed Camille on the lips.

Camille was confused and pushed him gently away.

Mister Higgins was smiling. "One, I've always wanted to kiss the cherry lips of a black woman. Thank you."

Camille couldn't help but smile. "And two?"

"I'm going to save your life. Step aside. If we have to leave, I can't run more than a few steps, but I can lead them away. Please."

She stepped aside when she heard the back door crash to the floor and could see the shadows as the zombies entered the house.

Mister Higgins strolled past her, as if he was going for a nice walk in the park, butter knives held high, and opened the door.

He rushed out, slicing his arms back and forth, knocking the first few zombies down. Others behind tripped, and there was a gap in the horde, which Mister Higgins filled as he pushed and kicked his way to the left.

Away from the open door.

The zombies followed him.

Camille heard the noise from the kitchen as the monsters tried to get into the house in search of human flesh.

She sprinted out the front door and angled to the right, throwing punches as she moved. Most of the zombies were being led away by Mister Higgins, who wasn't too fast at his age but still quicker than the undead.

Camille had to dodge a group of them. As long as she could keep space between herself and the zombies, she thought she had a chance.

They would overwhelm her by sheer number or by pushing her into a corner.

Camille looked back, trying to see if Mister Higgins was still alive, but there were too many zombies. Some of them were now completely focused on her, too.

She dodged the grasping hands ahead of her, moved left and right like she was a running back on a football field.

Camille needed to get down the block and as far away as she could.

She wondered what Pork Chop would think if he ever came home.

He'd see the destroyed kitchen, the open front door. No sign of his wife.

Camille kept moving, but more and more zombies were appearing on her path to freedom.

The woman had passed out once she'd fallen over the fence. Grady lifted her up and took her inside.

He put her down on the couch and checked her for wounds, she was dirty but not hurt as far as he could see.

Lovely, too. Maybe half-Asian. Filipino? To Grady it was all the same, and he called them Asian. What did it matter? He'd checked off a box for his harem.

She was around twenty-five, although it was hard for him to get a good gauge with all the dirt and filth on her body.

Grady found zip-ties under the kitchen sink and decided to run her a bath. She looked like she hadn't eaten in a couple of days, too. Maybe dehydrated.

"I'll treat you right, my little Asian princess," he whispered in her ear before carrying her to the bathroom.

He stripped her down, admiring her naked form. Running the bath water, he zip-tied her arms behind her back and put her in the tub.

She was breathing but not awake. He would never do anything she didn't want. Grady didn't think he was an animal.

In time they'll all realize I am their protector, and I alone can help them to live, he thought.

He'd collected a lot of different shampoos and conditioners from other houses. Perfumes and body sprays, too. She'd be nice and clean and smell good after he washed her.

Grady had finished, dried her off, and found a pair of red silk panties that almost fit her, lying her in bed and using another zip-tie for her ankles. He'd need to find handcuffs, which would be so much easier.

He was making tea, happy the power was on again when he heard her moan.

Grady made sure to have a big smile on his face when he went into the bedroom.

"You're awake. Good. Rest easy. You've been through a lot in the past few days. I'm making us tea, since your people like it," Grady said.

"Hawaiians?"

Grady laughed. "Everyone likes tea. Would you like some toast and butter?"

She nodded.

He went back to the kitchen, impressed she seemed to be taking this so well so far.

As he put two slices of bread into the toaster and found butter in the fridge, he heard her begin to squirm on the bed.

"Hey, why am I tied up? What are you doing to me? Where are my clothes?" She was cursing a lot now, too, but Grady ignored it. In time, she'd realize she was making a big mistake and apologize.

Because her hands were behind her back, Grady propped her up in bed with pillows and fed her. Gave her sips of tea.

She asked a lot of questions, but Grady shook his head. "Eat.

Drink. There will be time to figure it all out later. Right now you need to gather your strength. It's a different world."

He didn't know if he could trust her alone in the bedroom but knew she wasn't going to escape.

Satisfied he'd begun to gather his women, Grady went into the living room and opened the blinds.

And then he saw Camille running down the road, being chased.

Grady opened fire, shooting zombies about to drag her down. He made sure to clear a space around her, hoping not to accidentally shoot his dream woman.

"This way," he yelled to her and kept firing the rifle.

She headed in his direction and Grady fired and fired until he was out of ammo, picking up the next weapon. He made sure not to clear a path for her to go anywhere but toward him.

No sense in wasting ammo and then losing her.

"Hey, Camille," Grady said, letting her get behind him as he fired at the zombies.

"Grady? Your family is looking for you," Camille said.

He chuckled. "Are they? I wonder why. I have no use for them." He turned and faced Camille. "You're my family now."

"Huh?" That was all Camille got out before Grady slammed the side of her head with the rifle butt and knocked her out.

He dragged her body inside, the zombies a few steps behind.

Grady locked the door and pulled the blinds.

He stared at Camille and grinned.

Two in one day, within a couple of hours of each other, Grady thought. *If there is a God, he is looking down on me today.*

The epiphany hit Grady like a sledgehammer.

There was no God above.

Grady was the God, here on this Hell on earth.

He got out the zip-ties for Camille.

15

Isabella and Jarrod stood near the back door, waiting for it to burst open and fill the diner with zombies.

Instead, the door was unlocked with a key and pushed open slowly.

"Hello?"

Pork Chop and Louise stepped inside, and mother and daughter hugged. Drew had been in the office as backup and rushed to join his family.

Jarrod closed the back door and relocked it. "Anyone else out there?"

"No one breathing," Pork Chop said. "In here?"

Jarrod shook his head.

"Let me get you some pie," Isabella said to her mother.

"Pie sounds great," Pork Chop said.

They sliced up another apple and another cherry pie and passed out the pieces, everyone quietly eating as they stood around the kitchen.

The banging in the front of the diner had increased.

"We got inside right on time." Pork Chop wiped his mouth with the back of his hand. "A lot of them were filtering around the building."

Jarrod glanced to the front. "They're pressing against the door and windows. They'll be inside very soon."

As if on cue, the pounding on the back door began as the zombie pressed against the back of the building.

"Do we have weapons?" Louise asked.

Isabella shook her head. "We could break apart some chairs and use the legs, but we don't have firepower."

"Then we use the legs," Drew said. "Anything from dad?"

"Or my wife?" Pork Chop asked.

Everyone shook their heads.

As Drew started to break up the chairs, a couple of the windows cracked and glass spilled into the diner.

"We're almost at the breaking point," Jarrod said. He took legs from Drew and passed them out. "I say we make our stand in the kitchen. As long as the back door holds. Fight backward into the office if need be."

Pork Chop and Jarrod stood side by side behind the counter, with Isabella in the doorway to the kitchen. Louise and Drew were in the kitchen, watching the front and back.

Long minutes passed. The windows were busted open, and at first, it looked like zombies would be force-fed into the diner, but mostly they were sliced up on the broken, jagged glass still intact.

The front door's glass was shattered, but the items they'd put up as a blockade were still holding.

"Hold steady," Jarrod said, the chair leg in his hands shaking.

The front door began to slowly swing open, and zombies were starting to squeeze through. Pork Chop ran over and began clubbing the zombies, but it didn't have much effect. By the time Jarrod went over to help, several zombies had fallen through the open windows and were beginning to rise again.

Isabella ran over to help, but a zombie grabbed her by the ankle and dragged her to the floor. Isabella screamed when sharp teeth dug into her exposed neck.

Pork Chop was knocked down as the pile against the door fell onto him, and before he could rise, zombies fell upon him.

Jarrod turned to run but smacked right into two zombies, and he screamed as they bit into both of his arms.

Drew and Louise gave one another a look and turned to run into the office and bar the door, but the back door was ajar.

A zombie stepped inside the kitchen of the diner and seemed to be leering at the mother and her son.

It was followed by dozens more.

The military had never come to rid this part of the city of the zombies. Every couple of days there might be a helicopter flying overhead, but nothing on the ground.

Grady had used vehicles to block off the streets, circling his new palace about half a mile in all directions.

He'd found military trucks in a Publix parking lot and managed to take them all back to his home. He stored weapons in the living room and kitchen, away from his thirteen new wives.

Wearing a hazmat suit, Grady used shovels to scoop up some of the body parts to dispose of them. A block away, a house had burnt to the ground. He'd restart the fire and dump the bodies onto it, using whatever wood he could find as fuel.

He knew he'd need a bigger home, but right now it was all he had to control. Having thirteen women tucked into two small bedrooms wasn't the answer.

The electricity and water had gone completely now, but there was a river a couple of blocks away. He'd chain up one of the women and take her to fill milk jugs with water every few days.

Camille was with him when a man stepped out from behind a nearby house and waved.

Grady nodded at him before raising his rifle and firing three times into the man's chest. He didn't need a rival.

Camille looked like she wanted to talk but knew better now. It had been months since Grady had asked anything of the women except for his carnal needs and help gathering food and water.

He'd wandered most often by himself, stripping every house and business of anything he could use. The houses on either side of his and across the street were filled with his spoils.

Maybe I'll add to my house and build an addition, Grady thought but knew it made no sense. The noise would attract zombies as well as survivors.

Camille was bent down, filling a bucket with water from the stream, when Grady heard the noise, low at first.

A helicopter was approaching from the east, which meant from the nearby military base. They were out doing recon again, looking for zombies or the living.

Grady had no interest in being part of the rest of the world. Not when he had it so good on his own.

"Time to go," Grady said. He'd set up what looked like an old shed nearby, so they could hide and not be caught in the open in the event of air surveillance. Like right now.

The chain leading from his hand to the waist of Camille was pulled tight, and he turned to see if she was stupidly going to make a break for it. Not that she'd get far. The chain itself was thick, the lock around her the final nail in that coffin. He had the only key in his pocket.

Camille had faked Grady out, though, and instead of running, she was in his face.

Rather, the bucket was in his face. She slapped him across the head with it.

He didn't pass out, but he saw stars, and he fell to the ground.

Camille kicked him in the crotch three times, and then he blacked out.

Grady groaned and rolled over, spitting out dirt in his mouth.

"Don't move," he heard someone close to him say.

Grady saw many sets of military boots as he blinked and tried to smile.

He spit out a tooth.
Camille, grinning, was standing behind several armed men.
"There are a dozen more," Camille said. "You should really kill him now. He's no use to the new way of things, I imagine."
Grady hoped she was wrong. He slowly stood on shaky legs.
Two of the soldiers glanced at one another.
Grady closed his eyes.

DANCE WITH THE DEAD

ERIN LOUIS

1

MAYBE I SHOULDN'T be surprised that I am where I am. I mean I dropped out of school, totally ignoring my parents. My father especially. Mom was a little easier going about the whole thing, but honestly, I think she was just a little jealous. Not in a middle school, mean girl jealous way, but a clandestine covert kind of jealous. But it probably doesn't matter anymore. I'm on my way to who knows where, and I don't know if I'll even see them again. But I'm pretty sure if I had stayed in college, I'd be sitting in a cushy office somewhere, drinking Starbucks and talking down to my assistant.

But no. Here I am, driving a strip club manager's ten-year-old BMW, talking into a burner phone I picked up on my way out of town, because the radio won't work. I'm not sure who or if anyone will ever even listen to this. I might just delete it when I get to wherever I'm going. *Feeling cute, might delete later, ha ha.* But I can't handle the silence right now. Plus if I get picked up by the police, I'll have the fresh details. There won't be any point in lying then. And maybe relaying what just happened might help get my thoughts straight so I can figure out just what I'm going to do next.

I went in to work last night just hoping to make my rent. Just a stupid boring Wednesday night at the strip club. Risky Business is at least better than most of them around here. Although it's kind of out in the middle of nowhere. But it's close enough to the airport that we get lots of out-of-town guys. Most of the time I make much more than I would have had I stayed in college. I was supposed to be a business major. I bet I learned much more about business as a stripper though. Even more about middle-aged horny men. I wasn't planning on stripping forever, just a couple of years. Save some cash, sow a few oats, have some fun, then go back and get my degree before succumbing to the corporate world. I suppose even now I could go back to school. I got a trunk full of cash. I wouldn't even need a loan. Ha!

When I walked in last night, Lenny the manager was spun out as usual. He was my favorite manager, despite his prolific coke habit. The other managers were kind of dicks most of the time. I just avoided them. But Lenny could be personable, especially when he was high. Which was always. He greeted me like normal when I walked in. Wiping his nose before waving at me and grinning with his toothy smile. His graying brown hair stuck up, like he had been sweating and running his hands through it. High as a kite. I wonder if things may have turned out a little different had he been able to keep his nose out of the blow for just a little while.

I passed the DJ booth on the way to the dressing room and gave a curt nod to Charlie the DJ. A big stoner that guy, but I'll take a stoner over a cokehead any day. There were only a few dancers in the dressing room when I walked in. Lexi, my least favorite was there. My stripper nemesis. She was sitting in her spot. The choice one, out of the way of the blowing air conditioner vent. The managers always kept it slightly above freezing in there to make sure we didn't hang out in there too long. They wanted us out on the floor entertaining the customers.

Lexi was sitting in her cesspool of glitter. Everyone called her the Glitter Queen behind her back. She was obsessed with the stuff. It was in her lotion, which got all over the stage by the way. I slipped and fell on my ass once when I had to go on after her. She made her own body spray with her essential oils and of course, glitter. She knew I didn't like her, and the feeling was mutual. Although as much as I hated her, I hated glitter even more. It's the plague of the strip club. She sneered at me as I sat down to get ready.

I got dressed like usual, or undressed, but when I went to get up to check in with Charlie and get on the dance list, my shoe stuck to the carpet. I looked at the bottom of my platform heel and saw a glob of chewed gum smashed onto it, sparkling with glitter and fake hair. But as I scraped it off with my fingernail, I noticed that my heel had worn down to the metal post. That would turn out to be a blessing later, but last night I was afraid I would get in trouble if it scratched the stage. How totally dumb is that?

Ava and Kelly were there and I said 'hi' to them as I left the dressing room. I was cool with both of them. Ava was blond like

Lexi, but not as pretty. She was soft spoken and we didn't talk much. Kelly was going to school to be a nurse or something. She was just a bit on the thicker side and had flaming red hair. She was sweet as pie, and I bet she would have made a great nurse.

I passed Roxy on the way out the door to the main floor. She was just about to go on stage. I liked Roxy. Probably the only girl there I could call a friend. She was gorgeous with her dark skin and hair, but wasn't a snot about it.

Charlie smiled when I checked in and said, "Hey Tiff. In the mood for anything special tonight?"

"Yes. Hundred-dollar bills," I said. It was our usual banter.

He was the only one I let call me Tiff. My name is Tiffney, and I'm pretty sure I was the only girl at the club who used her real name. All the guys thought it was fake anyway. When they inevitably asked my real name, I liked to tell them it was Bubbles or Kitty. I know . . . I'm a card.

It was only 8pm and the club was still pretty empty. Eric, one of the two bouncers working, was on top of a ladder in the middle of the main floor. Messing with the disco ball they had installed last week. The main room wasn't that big, it only held around a hundred people or so. The disco ball, when it worked, sparkled and reflected the lights from the stage throughout the whole space. It gave the room a funhouse vibe. Especially if you threw in the hideous carpet with its random splotches of color. Ugly as sin, but it hid the wads of discarded gum and puke stains. The building was a bar before it was a strip club, and although smoking was banned at least ten years ago, the stink of cigarettes-past clung to the walls. A few other dancers were scattered around the room.

I scanned the main floor for a customer. There were a few guys. One table had three blue-collar-looking types, construction workers probably. A couple of dilapidated old farts that were regulars. But ones that didn't buy lap dances from me. There was one dude at the stage, watching Roxy do her thing. I was getting discouraged. But then I saw someone sitting by himself way back in the corner. I started to walk over. Lexi had come out of the dressing room and had seen him too.

We looked at each other. Well . . . I looked. She scowled. And started to walk quickly toward the lone customer. This was a frequent occurrence in the club. Two dancers aiming for the same guy. Like a half-naked game of chicken, one of us was going to have to break. I was slightly faster and closed the gap before Lexi. She turned away, but not before giving me one last dirty look. I smiled at her before turning that smile to the guy sitting alone in the dark.

"Hello beautiful," he said.

He looked like the perfect customer, and I had a good feeling about him. Perfectly groomed and nicely dressed in a light gray suit. I liked to work the weeknights precisely for guys like this. In town for business, and lonely, a guy like this could buy dances all night. My mom always told me to go with my gut feeling. My dad told me to ignore them. I should have listened to my dad.

"I'm Tiffney," I said. "How are you doing tonight handsome?" I wasn't even lying. He was good looking. Although, his cologne was kind of strong. Not bad, but strong.

"I'm just wonderful. My name is Bob. Are you available for a VIP dance?"

The way he said his name made me think it was fake. I didn't think much of it at the time because guys gave fake names sometimes. Why . . . I don't know. If they're trying to be anonymous, it's pretty pointless. I'm likely to forget their names right after they tell me anyway. I just call everyone *Hun* or *Love*.

"It just so happens that I am," I said to him and winked. Or tried to, I don't think I've ever nailed the sexy wink.

I walked him to the small VIP room in the back of the building. Sid, the other bouncer, was standing at the entrance. Sid was huge. Like seven feet tall. Okay, maybe not that tall, but he towered over me even in my six-inch heels. His bald head and long bushy beard would have made him look intimidating even without being a giant. He nodded as we walked in.

The VIP room is darker than the main floor. The tiny lights provided just enough light for me to see Lexi in the farthest corner dancing for one of the construction workers in my favorite booth. There were only about ten booths in all, and I liked that one because it was out of view of the cameras. It was everyone's favorite booth. If you wanted to break a rule or maybe slip an extra bill out of some guy's wallet, just the jerks I swear . . . no one would know. Well, Sid might, but he would keep his mouth shut if you slipped him an extra tip.

I sat Bob down just as the next song started so I didn't have time to talk to him. I wonder if I would have changed my mind and left if I had. Probably not though. He just looked like he wanted to spend money. He also looked sweaty, that should have been my first clue. But I was going with my gut. Like I said, I should have listened to my father.

I took off my top and started to dance. Lap dancing isn't really like dancing. I don't even know why they call it dancing. I climbed on top of him and started rubbing my boobs in his face. His cologne was overpowering, but it wasn't until I got up on him that I figured out why. Under that thick cologne was a different smell. A sickly one, only slightly hidden by the woodsy musk he was wearing. It reminded me of when we found a dead mouse in the pantry that had been there a couple of days. That sweet smell of decay. But there was something else. Dense BO, the kind usually reserved for the blue-collar types. The odor of a hard day's labor and not enough deodorant.

His stench was threatening to bring up my lunch, so I got up off him and turned around. With my butt in his lap, I had a chance to gulp some fresh air. I swear Charlie was playing the longest song ever, I knew it was the same length as all the other ones, but it felt like forever. They cut all the songs at the same length no matter what so each customer gets his money's worth.

But when the song finally ended, Bob said, "Keep going."

Something was weird about his voice. Like his mouth was full of gravel. I should have stopped then and left. Well, I should have run out of the building. But how the *hell* was I supposed to know? And I wanted the money.

I couldn't stay with my back to him the whole time, so I turned around to face him again. That was when I knew I had made a huge mistake. His eyes had glazed over, and his head was resting against the velour-covered lap dance booth. He could've been sleeping, had his eyes been closed. He looked dead. I leaned in closer, yet another mistake. I didn't feel any breath. Or rather, I didn't smell his breath. I could no longer smell his cologne. Just death and something like hot garbage.

I started to back away, just as he lunged at me.

2

I almost fell backwards. Good thing I was so steady on my heels. When Bob came out of the booth at me, he overshot and landed face first into the almost damp, but not quite filthy carpet. Sid saw what was happening and rushed over, but didn't get there in time. Bob reached forward and caught my ankle with his immaculately manicured fingers. He pulled me to the ground and right before Sid could grab him, he bit me.

Like *bit* me. I've had some crazy customers, but I've never had one bite me. I've even bitten a few on request, but this was a first.

Sid grabbed him by the hair on the back of his head and lifted him up off the ground. Bob didn't say a word. He flailed and twisted with his feet off the ground. It would have been funny, had I not been bleeding. The look on his face as he swung from Sid's fist was terrible. His eyes were the worst. Milky and unfocused, the dude was enraged. And I hadn't even told him how much he owed yet.

Sid got a second hand on him, but even at his size, he couldn't quite control him. Finally, he called out for Eric, unable to use his radio he had to yell. Eric was there in seconds. I watched from the floor as the two bouncers wrestled Bob out of the VIP room.

I got up carefully and went back to the booth to retrieve my top. But when I saw Bob's wallet on the seat, I picked it up. I opened it and removed the bills before stuffing it between the cushions. I keep a band around my ankle that I can fold bills into. I guess I should be thankful Bob caught the other one. Considering I hadn't been paid, and I was bleeding, I didn't care if the theft was caught on the camera. Under these circumstances, I didn't think the managers would care.

My ankle didn't hurt as I walked out of the VIP room. But it was bleeding and I needed to clean it. I didn't see Sid, or Eric, or Bob as I went back into the dressing room. Only Kelly was in there. I sat down and she saw the blood.

"Ooh. What happened?"

"Some customer attacked me. He fucking bit me. It was wild. I think he was sick or something. It doesn't hurt though."

She walked over, "Let me see."

Kelly grimaced as she saw the teeth marks and got up to go to her locker. She had a small first aid kit. It did hurt a little as she cleaned it with an alcohol wipe.

"I'm out of antibiotic ointment, but you should put something on it."

I looked around and saw Lexi's homemade body spray.

"How about that stuff. It's got all her special herbs and spices," I said.

"I don't think there's much to that essential oil stuff, but there are a few with some antibiotic properties. Give it a try, just clean it out when you get home and watch for an infection."

"You got it Doc," I said smiling.

"Yeah, not a doctor. Just a CNA. I'm just learning to wipe old people's butts and prevent bedsores."

I snatched up the bottle and squirted some of the glittery liquid on my ankle, but Lexi walked in just as I was setting it back down.

"What the fuck Tiffney?" she screeched. Kelly ran out the door, hard to blame her.

"Ugh, sorry. I got a little cut and was hoping your special brew might help," I said as sweetly as I could. But I think I sounded way more sarcastic than I meant to be. Or at least as I meant to sound.

"Keep your hands off my shit."

She wasn't wrong by the way. It is a huge breach of stripper etiquette to touch someone else's stuff. But it was one squirt of body spray for God's sake. I didn't say anything else and just left her to stew in her anger and glitter.

I stopped to talk to Charlie, but he was in the middle of announcing Ava to the stage, so I just walked past him instead. He was playing her favorite song, some old R&B jam I couldn't stand. I was going to look for another customer to dance for to help me forget about Bob, but I saw Lenny in the corner with Eric and Sid. Sid was lying down on one of the large couches that sat against one wall. Eric was hunched over him, while Lenny watched and clenched his jaw.

In yet another mistake, I walked over to see what was up.

"Is he ok?" I asked of Lenny.

"That fucked up customer bit him good. That guy was really drunk."

That guy wasn't any kind of drunk, I almost said. I *almost* said he bit me too but didn't. Telling them I was bitten might make it seem like I thought I was in some kind of zombie movie, and they would think I was nuts, or on dope. I saw then that both Eric and Sid were covered in blood. Eric was holding a towel to Sid's arm, but Sid didn't seem to notice. He looked unconscious. Some of the blood must have been Sid's but no way that all of it was. They looked like extras in a horror film. I figured the rest of the blood must have been Bob's. Both Eric and Sid were notorious for getting rough with unruly customers. Although this was a little excessive.

"Did you call the police?" I asked, stupidly. Lenny wasn't going to call the police. Not with all the coke he did, not to mention all the blood. But I didn't know what else to say. Sid looked bad.

"Go back to work, Tiffney, and don't worry about it."

I was about to do just that, when Sid got up. He moaned, and when he opened his eyes, they had the same milky film like Bob's had. I smelled the familiar noxious odor coming from his mouth. This time though, I ran.

I didn't look back as I sprinted for the DJ booth. But I heard Eric cry out as Sid attacked him. I jumped up on and into the booth where Charlie was bent over his soundboard, oblivious to what was happening. I looked back and saw Eric on the ground with Sid on top of him. If it wasn't for the blood, I might have thought they were play fighting. Sid had his head down and looked to be biting the back of Eric's neck. When he lifted his head up, he had a mouth full of *I don't even want to know what*, and Eric had stopped screaming. Lenny was just hopping up and down with his hands over his mouth.

Charlie finally looked up, and his half-lidded bloodshot eyes widened. His mouth dropped open and the unlit joint that had been between his lips fell out. Lenny stopped jumping and started running toward us with his hands waving.

"Get upstairs to the office," he yelled.

Charlie bent down to retrieve his joint and ushered me out of the DJ booth and through the swinging door that led to the hallway. Ava was still dancing away on stage. Lexi poked her head out of the dressing room as we passed and headed up the narrow stairs that led to the manager's office.

"What the hell?" she asked.

"Get upstairs now," Lenny barked.

Lexi came out, and Roxy was right behind her. The five of us ran upstairs, with Lenny in the lead. He opened the door and we all filed in. He plopped down at his desk and began clicking the mouse while staring into the large computer screen.

"Fuck. Fuck. Fuck," he said.

We all just stood there quietly. Charlie pulled a lighter out of his pocket and lit the joint he had nearly lost. I waited for Lenny to stop him, but he didn't. I thought about Ava on stage, and was about to go get her but Lenny started to speak.

"Some wild shit is going down. We need to stay here. I locked down the club and sent a message to Big Mike." Big Mike is the owner. I don't know much about him, on purpose. I know that he is probably into some bad stuff. You don't get a name like Big Mike unless you're into some shady shit. "Charlie, you got your phone on you?"

Charlie stuck the joint in his mouth while he reached into his pocket for his phone. He handed it to Lenny, who promptly threw it hard against the wall. Lexi yelped when it shattered. Charlie said nothing, just took another hit off his joint. There was no point in asking the dancers if they had their phones. We were all wearing bikinis, except for Lexi who was in a pink sparkly bra and panties. So no pockets.

"No one is calling anyone. I got this shit handled. Sit tight," he said.

Lenny had exactly *nothing* handled. After a few more clicks of the mouse, he got up and went to a large, locked cabinet that stood against the far wall of the small office. It was only my second time up there. The walls were covered with posters of porn stars, and it stank of stale booze. Charlie's joint actually made the place smell better. He unlocked the cabinet and opened the doors.

Inside there were two big black mean-looking rifles hanging from a rack. There was a small safe, and Lenny twisted the combination on the dial. The safe door swung open and Lenny removed a large bag of white powder. Inside I could see a couple of large handguns and cash. Stacks and stacks of cash. He took out the bag and walked back to his desk. Lexi, Roxy, Charlie and I watched as he dumped the contents of the bag out onto his desk. Lenny then put his face in the pile of coke and snorted.

"Fuuuuuuckkkkk!!!!! I've always wanted to do that."

We heard a scream from downstairs. I wondered if it was Ava on stage. Lenny walked back to the cabinet and withdrew one of the rifles. He shouldered the weapon and turned to look at us. His eyes were clear, but cloudy. He was alert, but not all there.

"What's going on dude?" Roxy asked him.

"The fucking zombie apocalypse," Lenny said and cackled. "But don't you worry your pretty little head babe. Uncle Lenny's here to save the day."

If she was impressed, Roxy didn't say so. I certainly wasn't. I was terrified. Charlie snuffed out his joint, and stuck the roach behind his ear. It disappeared behind his black curly hair.

"What are you going to do?" I asked. Yet another stupid question.

"I'm going out there to kill the zombies. You guys just sit tight."

He walked over to the door, opened it and stepped out. Charlie stepped quickly to lock it behind him. We stood staring at it waiting for gunfire. When several seconds passed and none came, Roxy said, "He forgot to load his gun."

3

I know how it sounds. Zombie apocalypse. Totally crazy. I didn't believe it either. It's not like Lenny was the most stable of people either. But he was right, sort of. From the mouths of cokeheads come the truth I guess. If only cause his brain was spinning too fast to come up with something else.

After he left, I went to the desk and the computer. I had to brush some of the coke aside. I wasn't even a little tempted. I've never been into the stuff. The others gathered around me as I sat down. On the screen was one view of the main floor, it was in black and white but the picture was clear. Dark splashes of what was surely blood but looked like it could have been paint was all over the room.

From that view, I couldn't see the stage. I saw the bar at the main entrance and the tables at the back of the room and the entrance to the VIP room. I saw no people. A click of the mouse brought a picture of the dressing room. I saw Kelly inside. She was sitting at the make-up counter with a blank look on her face. She looked to have a bit of blood on her, but otherwise looked ok.

"Kelly's in the dressing room. Someone should go and get her," I said.

To my utter surprise, Lexi spoke up. "I'll go. I'll grab my phone while I'm there. We can call for help." At one time, I'm sure there had been a landline, but it was long gone.

Lexi, aka the Glitter Queen, was proving not to be the total bitch I had made her out to be. I wonder if things had turned out differently we might have been friends. Before I had a chance to say anything, she was out the door and down the stairs. The rest of us watched the screen.

We saw her enter the dressing room and approach Kelly. And then we saw Kelly stand up and turn around to face her. The two stood face to face for a moment. We could see that Kelly was covered in blood from a large open wound in her throat. She then lowered her head and bit Lexi on the chest right above her right boob. We heard Lexi scream as she pushed the dead stripper away from her. Kelly was knocked backward onto the low counter, and the even in black and white, you could see the glitter on her bloody mouth and teeth.

Lexi was quick, and was out the door and up the stairs before Kelly could recover. We opened the door and let her back in. Kelly wasn't far behind, and we slammed the door in her face. She began to ram herself into it over and over. Shaking the wooden door in its frame. She hadn't been a large person, but she was sturdy. I hoped that the door was sturdier. Fear began to curdle the contents of my stomach and my knees started to quiver. But I stayed steady on my heels.

We helped Lexi sit down in one of the two faux-leather chairs on the other side of the desk. Roxy bent down to look at her bite.

"Hard to tell how deep it is through all that glitter," she said.

We all giggled in spite of ourselves. I swear as much as I disliked the chick, it wasn't in a mean way. We weren't laughing because it was funny, we were laughing because it was horrible.

"It doesn't hurt," Lexi said.

And I believed her. I had forgotten all about my own bite until then. It hadn't hurt all that much either. But it was then I started to wonder if it was a bigger deal than I had thought at first. That's how zombies work right? You get bit, you die and you start tearing people to bits in search of brains or something.

Charlie had gone to the cabinet, and was rummaging through it. He pulled out a first aid kit and brought it over. He handed it to Roxy, who unzipped it and pulled out a couple of things. As she cleaned and dressed the wound, Charlie and I went back to the camera. Outside the room, poor Kelly was banging away at the locked door.

The dressing room was now empty, so I clicked to the next screen. A view of the VIP room showed up. It looked to be empty also. I clicked again and saw the other side of the room. I was a little dismayed to see that everyone's favorite booth was in clear view of the camera. But that side of the room was empty too.

I clicked again, and got a view of the main room again. This one showed the stage. I saw the two old guys, the three construction workers and one dancer crowded around the stage. None of them throwing dollars. Okay bad joke. Sorry.

On stage there were four strippers surrounding the pole. There was no question they were dead. They were covered in blood, and one of them was Ava. I didn't recognize her from her face, as it was gone, but from the little flower tattoo she had on her ankle. It was the one piece of skin that wasn't shiny with blood. Tears burned in my eyes, but I held it together. We didn't see Lenny, but we saw his gun lying on stage.

"I cleaned it pretty good, but we should keep an eye on it," Roxy said. "I don't know if this is enough to turn her into one of them."

"I'm fine," Lexi said, trying to convince herself more than us.

"It seems to go pretty fast, so if it's going to happen, it should happen soon," Charlie added helpfully. Well sort of.

That was when I realized that my own bite might mean the same thing. I crossed my legs under the desk. I didn't want anyone to know that I had been bitten too. But I had already lasted much longer than the others who had been bitten by then. I was pretty scared though.

I went back to the screen and clicked again. This time I could see behind the bar. And Bob. Well, most of Bob. His head was missing. That was when I realized why Eric and Sid had been covered in blood. I knew that it was much more than if they had just beat the dude up. Which would have been par for the course.

"Oh wow," Charlie said.

"I think they must have cut his head off after the bastard bit Sid," I said. "Charlie, how many girls were on the list tonight?"

"Uh, about eight I think."

"Then I think we have them and all the customers accounted for. Pretty sure they're all dead."

I said that as I looked back at the view of the stage. "So I'm pretty sure it's zombies. I just can't see Lenny."

"Lenny said he locked down the club. I heard him talk before about an emergency switch somewhere in the club that shuts the whole place up tighter than a nun's butthole. I doubt he made it out. He probably just found a place to hide."

"I guess that means no one's getting in either," I said.

"From what I heard that's a good guess. Supposedly the lockdown switch alerts Big Mike, and I don't think anyone is getting in or out without him. So if we're getting out of here, we either wait for him or find the switch ourselves. In the ten years I've worked here I've never met the dude, and I don't want to."

I didn't want to meet the guy either, but at that point, I didn't know what else to do. The guns and the dope weren't a great sign. I didn't think it would be safe to assume that Big Mike would have our best interests in mind. Not to mention, there were no landlines in the office and the only phones we had were in the dressing room.

"Unless he's dead somewhere, I think we're the only ones left alive." I glanced at Lexi, who actually didn't look that bad.

I regretted saying that as soon as it came out of my mouth. Lexi put a hand to her chest and sighed. After all, I had been bitten too, and it could be me that started going after people next. Considering the time, that was more likely.

Kelly seemed to have stopped banging on the door.

Roxy had been quietly going through the cabinet. "We have one rifle left and two 9mm handguns. The rifle is an AR-15, and could probably take out all of those fuckers at once. I've only shot one once."

"I've never shot a gun at all," I said.

"Me neither," said Charlie.

We all looked at Lexi, who had some color back in her face. "I used to go to the range with my dad. I can handle a gun. In fact, I can handle the rifle."

"Well, I don't want to sit here and wait for Mike," Roxy said as she started to take out the guns and boxes of ammo.

She brushed the coke off the table and onto the floor, and laid out the guns and one really big knife.

"I don't like guns, I'll take the knife," Charlie said.

Lexi got up and started to load the rifle, while Roxy prepared the handguns. She showed me quickly how to load it and where the safety was. We must have made too much noise, because the banging started on the door again.

"Someone's going to have to handle Kelly first," I said and felt like a jerk. I said handle because I couldn't bear to say kill her. She was such a sweet girl.

I was trying not to think too much about all that stuff right then. It was so scary, but so sad. I had liked Kelly. And Sid, and Eric. Even strung out, Lenny wasn't that bad. Not to mention all the other people who had just come in last night to have a good time or make some money and go home. None of them deserved any of this.

I know most people look at strip clubs as dirty nasty places for deviants. I know my parents did. But they're just full of regular people. For the most part good people even. And at any rate, it's an honest place. Everybody that goes or works there knows the rest of society already thinks they're all scumbags. So the people who work there are like a weird little community, bound by stigma. A family of misfits.

"I know," Charlie said. "I will. I got the knife. I'll put her down easy when we open the door. I don't think we want the noise of the guns bringing the rest of them up here."

"Thank you," I said and I was grateful. "Let me check the cameras again, before we do this."

I wanted to make sure all the dead were still where I saw them last, but I was also trying to buy some time. I played a good game, but I was scared. Adrenaline was keeping me from really freaking out. It's only now starting to wear off. But then while we were all still alive in that little filthy office, I wanted a moment to make sure I was ready.

The VIP room was still empty, as was the back of the main room, and dressing room. I switched to bar view and studied it for a moment. Which was stupid, because it was still empty too. But I stared at it anyway, trying to buy a little more time. And saw Bob's head. It had rolled under a rack. Why did they have such clear cameras? Lower quality would have worked just fine for their purposes. But no. They had to put these HD high-tech cameras that allowed me to see all the details of Bob's ruined head. I could see each ragged shred of skin from his severed neck; it looked like they had used a steak knife. I could also see that his tongue was hanging out.

I leaned over to the side of the desk and threw up. I wiped my mouth and sat up. I closed my eyes for a minute for the nausea to pass. I clicked the mouse before I opened them again and saw the view of the stage. It looked exactly the same as when I looked at it last. The same four dancers clustered around the pole, all reaching up toward something.

I looked for a zoom function on the camera. When I found it, I zoomed in. I could see that there was something on the pole. The undead strippers were all reaching for it. I leaned in a little closer. And saw the bottom of Lenny's shoes.

4

"Guys? I found Lenny. He's at the top of the pole," I said.

Roxy and Charlie came over to see what I was seeing. Slowly we watched as more of him came into view. First both shoes, then his brown suit pants. The only things holding him up were the rubber soles of his shoes and the bare skin of his sweaty hands. Neither would keep him up very long. All strippers and probably most managers know that bare skin is what holds you on to the pole. Lenny didn't have much time. He was slipping as we watched.

"We need to hurry. He's the only one who knows where the switch is to unlock the doors," Charlie said.

He seemed to have perked up. We took our guns and walked over to the door. Charlie led the way, and put his hand on the knob. We held our breath and listened for Kelly outside. But it was dead silent on the other side of the door. Charlie looked back at us and raised his eyebrows to ask if we were ready. I don't think we were at all, but we all nodded.

Roxy was right behind Charlie, then Lexi, then me. The big ass gun was shaking in my hand. We heard Lenny scream downstairs, and Charlie opened the door. The landing was empty. So were the stairs. Charlie creeped out the door and motioned that it was safe. Roxy followed him out, holding her own gun like she knew what she was doing. Not like me, before all this I hadn't shot anything bigger than a Nerf gun.

We were quiet, but as we got down to the bottom of the stairs, Kelly came out of the dressing room. Charlie had been holding the knife out and ready to strike, but he must have been shocked for a second or two. Because Kelly grabbed his arm and yanked him in close. She bit into the soft part of his cheek. He swung the knife and connected with her skull. But this isn't the movies where a blade just slides in like it's going into grandma's Jell-O mold. Instead, it bounced off her head and out of his hand.

He pushed her free, but she took a chunk of his face with her. Roxy pointed the gun at her head, but Lexi put a hand on her arm to stop her. Lexi picked up the knife that Charlie dropped and pushed Kelly face first onto the floor. Holding the back of her head, she stuck the knife between her skull and neck and into Kelly's brain. She immediately stopped struggling.

Lexi stood up and shook the blood off the blade. Still in her stripper heels, and covered in blood, she looked like a pink glittery warrior. Seriously, in that moment I had a whole new respect for the Glitter Queen.

We turned our attention to Charlie, who wasn't doing okay. He was holding his face, but his hand wasn't doing much to stop the blood. It leaked through his fingers. We helped him into the dressing room and sat him down. Roxy grabbed a pair of panties hanging from a chair nearby and pressed it to the wound. I wondered for a minute if they were clean, which of course mattered not at all. My brain comes up with some arbitrary shit in a panic.

Roxy plucked the snubbed-out joint from the DJ's ear and put it in his mouth. I looked around and found a lighter on one of the counters. I lit the tip. He took a big hit as Roxy held the blood-soaked panties to his face. His eyes closed as he drew in, but when he opened them, we could see he wasn't going to last long.

They hadn't gone all milky just yet, but they looked dimmer. He coughed. The blood coming from his face was slowing down. Oozing instead of pouring from his cheek. Charlie was a good dude. Always nice, I'd never seen him be a dick to anyone. Not even to the girls he privately confessed he didn't like.

His eyes closed, but they didn't open again. He slumped and began to slide out of the chair. Roxy and I guided him to the floor. I heard Lexi let out a quiet sob, but only one. She came over to us and didn't say a word as she helped us turn him over onto his stomach. We didn't know how long we had until he got back up again.

Lexi pressed the tip of the knife into the soft spot between his spine and skull, just as she had with Kelly. She gave one hard push, and the blade found his brain. We just sat there for a minute. The three of us cried silently. We didn't hear anything from the main room, so we sat there for a few moments. I really liked Charlie too. Dammit. We all did.

"How are you feeling Lexi?" Roxy asked, breaking the silence with the question we all were thinking.

Lexi looked like she was going to answer with one of her patented sneers, but her face softened, and she said, "I feel fine. But I get it. It doesn't make sense. I should be face down on the floor too." She fingered the wound on her chest. Which still sparkled with glitter, but otherwise was just bloody teeth marks.

"I mean this whole deal doesn't make any sense. But we know for sure that it started with Bob. And he ain't talking," I said and giggled. Roxy and Lexi both rolled their eyes at me, which I totally deserved. But in my defense, it was a hysterical giggle, not like I was laughing at headless Bob.

"Well, you seem okay for now. Let's figure out how to get out of here. I think we need Lenny. If he's still up on the pole," Roxy said.

"You guys ready?" Lexi asked. At least I wasn't the only one asking stupid questions, I mean who the hell is *ever* ready to kill zombies.

I wasn't quite ready, and I remembered that we were in the dressing room. Where our phones were. I ran to my locker, opened the door, and pulled out my phone.

"Hey, my phone is in here." I held it up to show it to the other girls, but when I looked at it, it had no service. "Shit."

"Let me guess," Roxy said. "No service?"

I nodded. Lexi had already retrieved her phone. She held it up to see that it had no service either.

"When Lenny locked down the club, it probably blocked the cell signals too. There's enough dope, guns and cash to send Big Mike and all his minions to prison for a long time. I'm not sure exactly what his deal is, but he's not dicking around. We need Lenny. Get your shit together ladies, let's go." Roxy picked up her gun and moved toward the door.

I picked up my gun and we stepped quietly out of the dressing room and into the hallway. Lexi picked up her rifle and gave us the nod that she was all set. She stepped into the lead and moved toward the swinging door. We listened there for a moment.

I don't know what I expected to hear. Moaning and shuffling I suppose, but we heard nothing. We waited just a moment longer, and heard a low grunting sound. I thought it was the bodies at first, but when I listened closer, it sounded like Lenny. He was slipping.

Lexi opened the door, and the damn thing squeaked on its hinges. The music had stopped playing sometime while we were up in the office. The door had probably been squeaking for a while, but there was always music in the club, we never heard it until just then. The worst time ever.

Eric was right on the other side. On a normal night, we'd have told him about the squeaky hinge and he would have been there with a can of WD40. But as you have probably guessed, he wasn't trying to fix the squeak. He reached out one hand, which was missing a finger, toward Lexi. Her gun was too long and he was too close for her to shoot him, but she fired off a round anyway. It hit the disco ball, which swung but didn't fall.

I heard a loud bang behind me and watched Eric's head disappear in front of me. His body dropped to the floor with a thud. Like the knife in the skull, I guess I thought that there would be a small round hole in the head when someone got shot. That was not it. Maybe it was the type of gun or bullet or something, but Eric's head was there one second. And the next it was gone in a red blur. *Oh god. I'm never ever going to get that out of my head.*

The rest of the bodies started coming then. The ones on the floor around the stage shuffling toward us. Lexi opened fire. She was much better with the knife than the rifle. Her aim was awful. She wasn't as experienced as she had made herself out to be. But then again strippers are pretty good at faking it. So maybe I shouldn't have been surprised. I probably shouldn't be talking shit though. I was still too scared to think about shooting my gun.

Lexi's first bullet spray came out in a burst. I don't know how many rounds were fired, but they all hit way too low. She took out a construction worker at the knees. He was still moving, but much lower to the ground. A dead dancer was hit in the gut, which barely slowed her down. But Roxy got her with one shot to the head. I never got to ask her where she learned to shoot.

The zombie strippers on stage had left Lenny and the pole to come after us. Miraculously, they all still had their shoes on. They tottered toward us from the stage. They each fell off one by one face first. Lenny slid down the pole.

Lexi and I hopped up over the chairs around the tip rail and onto the stage. It seemed like the safest place, as neither of the dead customers seemed to know how to use the steps anymore. Roxy shot one of the old regulars directly in the face, and jumped up with us.

"Big Mike will be here any minute, I'm sure of it," Lenny huffed.

There were about ten or so zombies left, and they made their way back to the edge of the stage. One of the dead girls, I think her name was Sophia, reached for me with the one arm she had left. I kicked her away and was about to shoot her, but I hesitated and Roxy shot her in the face. I swear I thought I was tougher than that. Sophia's face blew out the back of her head, and I turned to puke again. I fought it off though, and held it. Not a big win, but just then I was taking what I could get.

Lexi put down the rifle and held out her hand for my gun. I looked down and handed it to her. I wasn't any good with it obviously. One by one, Lexi and Roxy started to pick off our undead audience. Lenny and I leaned back against the mirrored backside of the stage and watched. I had the sense to be just a little embarrassed while two strippers saved us from the zombies. Lenny did not.

When they were finished, the whole place smelled like blood and gunpowder. But at least it didn't smell like puke. I had to give myself another pat on the back for that one. Our two half-naked heroes joined Lenny and me at the mirror. We all slid down and sat there looking out at the worst Wednesday night in the history of the *Risky Business* gentleman's club.

5

I had my eyes closed but opened them when Lenny spoke. "You guys didn't do all my coke did you?" Seriously, if we had, we'd be dead. It was a lot of coke.

"Yeah, no Lenny. We didn't," Lexi said and shot him one of her famous death looks. Like the sexy wink, I tried but didn't quite cut it.

Lenny pulled himself up and started to walk off the stage. We knew where he was going. He hopped down and made his way to the door that led to the office upstairs. He was going to be pissed when he saw that most of his blow had ended up on the floor. But right then he was on a mission. A mission that was almost ended when he tripped over one of the bodies that had greeted us when we came out to rescue him.

Lexi's poorly aimed spray of bullets had cut one of the patrons in half. The bottom half wore jeans and lay still. The top half had been still until Lenny kicked it in the head and fell face first into the carpet, which was filthy before, but now it was soaked in blood. The torso pulled itself along and reached out to Lenny who kicked it in the face again and laughed. He got up and trotted through the door. We could hear him bounding up the stairs.

"I guess we should follow him. He knows where the switch is to get us out of here. It's probably in the office," I said.

And at that time, it seemed logical that the switch was somewhere in the office with the guns and dope and cash. We got up to follow. All of us were still in our stripper gear, except for Roxy who had taken off her shoes at some point and was barefoot. I never took my shoes off in the club. Who knew what was on that damned carpet. Plus stripper shoes aren't nearly as uncomfortable as they look. The tall platform and heel are just an illusion of pain. They are actually very comfortable. I used to joke that I could run a mile in them. I thought I was exaggerating, but after last night, I know I wasn't.

By the time we got upstairs, Lenny was on the floor vacuuming it with his nose. Cocaine is a hell of a drug folks. A hell of a drug. His ass was in the air when we walked in. When he finally came up for air, he just sat on the floor. His eyes darting back and forth. He sniffed a few times. I had heard people talk of the Colombian Cold, but I didn't know what it meant until I heard him sniffing like that.

Lenny's eyes fixed on Lexi. Specifically her boobs. I was kind of pissed until I realized he wasn't checking out her goods. He was looking at the bite. His face grew dark.

"You're bit, little lady," he said, but it came out all mushy because his jaw was jerking so much.

Lexi's hand went to her chest, where the bite still didn't look that bad. She still looked okay too. Splattered in blood and some bits of something red but too chunky to be just blood, but she didn't look like she was getting sick. Roxy had her gun by her side, but she was quietly alert.

"You're going to turn. I'm sorry," he said and started to stand up.

He had lost his suit jacket somewhere and his tie hung sideways. His eyes were wild and he reached for Lexi. I didn't see him pick up the knife he now had in his hand. He lunged at her, but a shot rang out and he fell to the floor. He hit the desk as he fell and the large computer screen wobbled and then shattered when it hit the desk.

Roxy shot him in the leg. He screamed. Blood flowed like appletinis at a bachelorette party. Roxy took off her top and sat on the floor next to him. She tied her bikini top around his leg just above the knee to stop him from bleeding out.

I had misjudged the ladies I worked with. Roxy and I were buddies, but I had no idea of her skills with firearms and medical knowledge. She was a few years older than me and I didn't know much about her. I wonder if she had told me and I forgot. Either way, I was happy to have her there. I worked with a bunch of badass chicks and didn't even know it.

Lenny's screaming turned into whining.

"So where is the button to unlock the doors?" Lexi asked.

"You shot me." He was leaking tears, but I don't think any of us had much sympathy. "That bitch is about to turn and kill us anyway. You better put her down."

Lexi kicked him lightly in his wounded leg and he screamed again. She bent down, to get close to him. I think she was going to ask him about the switch again, but before she could, he stuck the knife, I think we all assumed that he had dropped, into the meaty part of her arm. She yelped, and backed away. Roxy shot him in the face.

"So thanks, but what the hell? We still need to get out of here. Hopefully before Big Mike gets here," Lexi said, holding her arm.

"He wasn't going to tell us," Roxy said. I don't know if she was right, but the dude wasn't in his right head, and didn't seem to be willing to cooperate anyway.

Lexi looked at her arm. It didn't seem to be a deep cut. It didn't even seem to be bleeding much.

"So, when all this started, Lenny was downstairs by the bar. He went from there with all of us up here. Do any of you remember him flipping a switch or anything?" I said.

"I don't," Roxy said.

"Me neither," Lexi said and she was already roaming about the little room looking for the switch.

We all joined her. I looked under the desk, but saw nothing. I was disappointed because that seemed like the most logical place to put such a thing. But nada.

We turned the place inside out, overturning chairs, ransacking drawers and cabinets. Destroying the place, like rockstars on bender in a cheap hotel room. Nothing was spared our wrath. We checked the closet and the little bathroom but came up with nothing. I gave up and sat down. Stumped. The other girls did the same.

It was still bugging me that Lexi had gotten bit, but hadn't turned. Okay, so it was bugging me that I had been bit. I was afraid to tell them, but since we were just sitting there and so far, Lexi was okay, I decided to confess.

"So guys, I was bitten too," I said and braced for them to freak out and shoot me. I held up my leg so they could see my ankle, which still glittered from Lexi's body spray. "I danced for the guy that started all this stuff. Bob, he freaked out and bit me. He bit Sid as him and Eric were trying to throw him out."

"And you haven't turned," Roxy said giving no indication she was going to blow my head off. I let out the breath I was holding.

"What happened to the guy?" Lexi asked.

"Eric or Sid killed him. He's behind the bar. They cut off his head. I think that's why Lenny wouldn't call the police and locked everything down. Well, one of the reasons," I said. "Fuck! The bar. Lenny must have hit the switch in the bar!"

We all bolted up and out of the office. Roxy led the way. When we got downstairs, she jumped over the half zombie who was gnashing his teeth at us as we passed.

I went behind the bar and began to look for the switch to no avail. Roxy and Lexi had no luck either. It seemed like we weren't going anywhere. But it had to be there so we kept searching desperately. We checked under the bar and in the little cabinets and I wanted to scream with frustration. Where the hell was it?

"Maybe it was on his phone or something, like a remote-control app?" Lexi said.

"I don't know. An app might leave a record or something. I think it's in the club," I replied.

We heard a shuffling, and all shut up to listen. The front entrance was on the other side of the wall behind the bar. We heard the doors open, and a couple of faint voices. Big Mike was here.

And he wasn't alone. I peered my head around the bar to look. And I have no idea why they called him Big Mike. He's not a big anything. There's no way he was more than five foot. It must be like when you name a huge guy 'Tiny' or something. He wore a faux-leather jacket that I'm guessing he thought made him look tough. But he looked like a little kid in tough-guy costume.

The two dudes he had with him were extra-large though. They looked every bit the part of the typical mobster goons. One of them had a big lumpy bald head and he wore a dark-colored T-shirt that was several sizes too small. His broad shoulders were barely contained by the thin fabric. The other guy had a blond crew cut that framed a freakishly small face. The size of his head dwarfed his features. His wife beater was stained with what I thought was blood, but I think it was food. Neither of them looked like they held MENSA cards.

They padded into the club quietly. Big Mike looked at them with a finger to his lips. He looked around the room surveying the damage. He didn't even look shocked by the carnage. I still don't know what shady shit he was into. Obviously, guns and drugs, but he didn't look like a mob guy, or gang member. Just this weird little, almost mythical, dude who everybody seemed afraid of. I don't think Big Mike could scare anyone on his own though, he looked like a strong fart would blow him over.

I lost sight of the three of them as they walked around the bar and toward the DJ booth. I didn't hear anything for a minute or two, until the half-a-customer started to moan.

"Hey Mike, look at this." I heard one of the goons whisper. I thought because he had the sense to whisper that he might not have been as dumb as he looked, but then he said, "Ha! This dude doesn't have any legs!"

"Shut up." I heard Big Mike say whispering too. "Put that down."

"Owww! It fucking bit me!" the goon said and this time didn't have the sense to be quiet.

I heard a squishy thud, as the guy dropped the body, and Big Mike say, "Get upstairs dumbass and be quiet for fuck's sake."

The door squeaked and I looked at Roxy and Lexi hunkered behind the bar with me. I nodded my head toward the front entrance, and they nodded back. I slowly raised up to look over the bar. The three men had headed upstairs. At least I was pretty sure they had. I motioned for them to stay put. I crept out and tip-toed around to the front entrance. I pushed on the door, but it wouldn't open. So I went back to the bar.

I had no idea how long those guys would be up there, but I was sure that they would come searching the bar next. I was petrified, but I didn't want to show it to the other girls. I didn't think it would shake either of them, but I didn't want them to think I was about to crumble. Although I was getting pretty close.

"They're going to come back here," I whispered.

Lexi whispered back, "Go to the VIP."

Roxy nodded and went first. We ran across the gore-covered carpet to the VIP room.

6

The VIP room was still deserted like I had seen on the camera. We went to the corner to talk and see if we could figure out a way out of there. We didn't think that Mike and his goons would be upstairs long. But for real, we were just bumble-fucking our way through all this. There was one exit in the VIP, but it had a sign on it that said an alarm would sound if we tried to open it. So that seemed like a bad move. Plus, we figured it was locked like the other door. The door in the VIP room and the main entrance were the only two exits in the whole building.

We gathered close to where I had danced for Bob, and I remembered that I had stuck his wallet in the cushions. I slipped my hand in there and pulled it out. I don't even know why I did it, but I had a feeling it could give us some information. So that time, mom was right.

I opened it and saw my suspicion confirmed. Bob was not his real name. It was Kurt. Which makes it even more stupid that he gave me a fake name. Kurt wasn't any less common than Bob. Guys are so dumb sometimes. Although, Kurt wasn't all that dumb it seemed. I went through the cards and stuff, and found some weird shit.

He had an ID card next to his wallet for some kind of lab. They made or tested some kind of chemicals. I don't know. There wasn't any money. I still carried the bills he had around my ankle. There were credit cards and random business cards. I found a business card for Big Mike, which I thought was super weird. I showed it to Roxy and Lexi. Lexi looked surprised, but Roxy didn't at all.

Up until then, Roxy and I had hung out little. We smoked some weed together, but I didn't know her all that well. I could see by the cagey look on her face that she knew something we didn't. But just then, we were focused on getting out of there. We had no working phones, no way out that we knew of, and three scary dudes upstairs. So, although I suspected that she had some information, I wasn't ready to press her on it. I figured she'd tell us when we needed to know.

I thought the wallet was empty, but then I saw a little yellow piece of paper hidden in the folds of the leather. I pulled it out and it was a sticky note with messy handwriting on it. It read, *Neutralizer = polyethylene terephthalate.* None of us had any clue what that was. And I wouldn't have known what that was even if I had stayed in college. I was trying to learn about business not chemistry.

"What the hell is that?" Lexi asked.

"I don't know, but I think we should hang on to it. If we think this through for a minute, Bob, I mean Kurt, looks like he was patient zero. He worked at some kind of chemical lab, so if he made whatever caused the zombies, maybe 'neutralizer' is the antidote?" Finally, I felt like I said something smart.

"That makes sense, I guess," Lexi said.

But you could see in her eyes that she was scared. And I knew that we were thinking the same thing. Whatever that chemical was on the sticky note, both of us had a good reason to find out what it was.

Roxy had her head down and was quiet for a few moments. When she spoke, she was almost whispering. We had to get close to hear her.

"I guess I should tell you guys something." She paused. "Big Mike and I had a bit of a thing for a while. He's a douche, I know. But I guess I was kind of intrigued. It was right after I started dancing. I've gotten much smarter. But back then, it seemed exciting. So obviously, he's into some bad shit. He has some connections with some really bad people. Like mobsters and shit. But he isn't one. Just a wannabe. He gets his drugs and guns from them, but I'm pretty sure they think he's a joke. Anyway, one night, this was a couple of years ago, we got fucked up on some expensive bourbon and he told me some stuff. That was the only time he ever talked about his business, but he was totally hammered. He told me that he hooked up with this doctor guy. And that they were working on some kind of new drug or whatever. He wasn't very clear. But he told me that the doctor guy was kind of a nut. Like crazy. That he was super smart but talked about the end of the world. Mike said he was weird with women. Like hated them. Talked about slutty women ruining the world. Just a weird man. Anyway, Mike was hoping that the guy would help him make this drug or something. I guess to sell. Like that TV show where the teacher makes meth. That was about it. It sounded like some stupid plan that wasn't going to go anywhere. I hadn't really thought about it, but I think this Kurt is the guy he was talking about. I also think that all this could have something to do with whatever they were making."

Lexi and I kind of just stared at her. It seemed a little nutty. But then again this whole thing was nutty. We were sitting in a VIP room going through some mad scientist's wallet talking about zombies and mobsters. Even so, we weren't all that sure how any of this would help. But I tucked the sticky note along with Kurt's money into the band around my ankle and hoped that I would have a chance to Google what was written on it.

Roxy went on, "I'm not exactly sure that the lockdown stuff is even real. I think it might just have been something he told people. I do know that he had something installed that could block the Wi-Fi signals coming into the building. But I bet the doors are unlocked. I also bet that's why Lenny didn't tell us about the switch. I don't actually think there is one."

"What the fuck, Rox? We could have been out of here by now," Lexi yelled. She had raised her voice and I was terrified that the bad guys might hear us.

"We have no keys, it's the middle of the night, we're half naked and this place is out in the middle of nowhere. Where exactly do you think we're going to go?" Lexi was quiet. "We need to find some car keys before we even think about trying to leave. If we walk out of here like this, those guys are going to find us and kill us."

She had a point. Lexi had forgotten her rifle behind the bar, and I wasn't even mad. This was an epic shit-show after all. But Roxy and I had held on to our guns. Roxy had a couple of bullets and I still had all of mine. So, we had that going for us, at least.

"Roxy and I still have our guns. If we can get to the dressing room, I can get my keys and we can sneak out of here," I said.

"Assuming we can get around those dudes upstairs. I didn't hear them come back down," Roxy replied.

Roxy tip-toed toward the entrance to the VIP room and poked her head around the doorway. After a moment, she looked back and motioned for us to come too. We padded over there. I was the only one still in my shoes. I probably should have taken them off, but I'm so glad I didn't. The main room was empty. It was quiet. Roxy stepped out and we followed her. We moved quickly and got to the door to the hallway that led to the dressing room when we heard the guys on the other side of the door. We hopped up onto the DJ booth, and out of the way.

Big Mike was talking. "Lenny fucked this all up. I told him not to let that crazy fucker into the club. Now look at it. Rob, did you get all that shit in place? Right at the support posts like I told you. If you misplaced any of those bombs, you'll fuck all this up worse. There needs by be nothing left of this building."

"I did boss. Can we watch?" The guy sounded like a little kid, waiting for a bowl full of candy.

"No asshole. I told you. We need to be as far away as we can. Go double check, Ed, help me get this shit to the car."

We heard the door squeak and saw one of the guys come through. The bald one,nso it was a nice, visible target. Roxy had her gun ready and pulled the trigger just as the guy's head came through. But she missed. She fucking missed and hit him in the shoulder. *Seriously*, this guy was built like a side of beef. I don't think he even felt it.

"Ed!" Mike yelled as he came through the door after him.

Lexi and I had crouched back into the DJ booth, but Roxy was still poised at the edge and pointing the gun. She got it to Big Mike's head and pulled the trigger, but it just clicked. The side of beef apparently named Ed grabbed her by the hair and pulled her out of the booth. I don't think he or Mike saw us hiding. I still had my gun, but I wasn't even thinking. I was so scared, oh my god. I was so scared.

Ed pinned Roxy on the floor. She was lying in a big pool of someone's blood. Probably more than one person's. Mike pulled out a little gun. I bet the twerp couldn't handle a bigger one. He pointed it at her head and Ed the beef guy stood up and smirked. I still can't believe they didn't notice us there.

"Who else is here Roxy?" Mike said.

"What the hell Mike. What's going on?"

"Nothing you need to worry about Sugar, that mad doctor guy started some shit. We're just cleaning it up. Now tell me, who else is here Rox, and where are they? Tell me and I'll take you with me before we blow this place to hell."

"They're in the VIP," Roxy said, and Mike pulled the trigger.

7

The DJ booth is up on a platform. It's usually dark except for the lights on all the controls and computer screens. Although, as it's right next to the door it was a good hiding place. As long as no one bothered to look up in it. Lexi and I were crouched down on either side of Charlie's stool, Mike and his two meatheads were totally unaware we were there.

All three of them started for the VIP room. They got about halfway there when I adjusted my position. Which should have been silent, but I brushed up against the stool. When I did, I knocked something off the top of it, probably one of Charlie's lighters. It dropped to the floor. In any other situation, such a sound would go completely unheard. But this was about the weirdest situation I could imagine. Without the constant ass-shaking music, every little noise sounded like cannon fire.

Big Mike turned around, but his goons kept going towards the VIP room. We had been hidden by the shadows, but the booth was wide open. He was looking right at us. Lexi whimpered. We were caught. Roxy was no more, and I was the only one with the gun. Well, if you didn't count Big Mike.

"Ed, go check out the VIP," Mike said as he and Rob came toward us.

Mike had his puny gun pointed at us. Rob didn't have a gun, but he did have fists that looked like whole hams. One of them held what was definitely a really big knife but looked like a toy in that dude's hand. Ed was bleeding from Roxy's bullet, but he didn't move like he was hurt at all.

I pulled out my gun, checked with my finger to make sure the safety was off, pointed and fired. I thought I was aiming at Big

Mike, but for real, it was my first time firing a gun. Like ever. It kicked back hard, and the bullet went up toward the ceiling. I didn't hit anyone. But I did hit the disco ball that Eric had been putting up when I got there last night. Well, not the disco ball itself but the part that connected it to the ceiling.

Mike had his gun trained on me but didn't get the chance to fire. The disco ball came crashing down. It landed square on the little bad dude. It shattered and Lexi screamed. I think I did too, but honestly, I don't remember.

Rob turned around and ran to his boss. Big Mike was a mess of mirrored glass and blood. Hitting the stupid disco ball was lucky as hell. But what was even luckier was the fact that Rob totally forgot about the gun that Big Mike had. I could see it a few feet away. A small black spot in the complicated pattern of the carpet. I tell you what, whoever designs the carpet in strip clubs is a master at camouflage.

Rob was cooing over the now-dead wannabe mobster and he seemed to have forgotten about Lexi and me. But Ed had heard the crash and came lurching out of the VIP room. I don't think he liked his boss that much because he lumbered right past Rob. Lexi and I stood up. There was no point in trying to hide now. Lexi held out her hand for the gun. I gladly handed it to her.

Ed got about ten feet away when she fired. She missed. This whole nightmare was a comedy of errors. Except I guess for the comedy. My favorite DJ was dead, as were all my friends. Seriously, if you had told me that one day I'd be stuck in a strip club fighting off mobsters and zombies with the Glitter Queen, I'd have wondered what kind of dope you were on. Like how in the hell does this even happen?

Ed kept coming. Lexi fired again and this time it caught him in the gut. But the guy just kept coming. One more bullet caught him in the chest and he fell. He rolled around on the floor like a dying fish. A huge dying fish. But Lexi's bullet must have torn him up good. Blood gushed out of him. I always heard gut shots could be really bad, and this one definitely was. He grunted and then started to make this sloppy gravelly sound when he exhaled. I almost felt bad for him, but he had been coming to kill us. Finally though, he went silent and limp. If this were a real zombie movie, we would have had to destroy his brain. But so far, only people that had been bitten got up again. So there's that.

Rob got up from the mess that was Big Mike. I think he was crying. But he was pissed, like super mega pissed. And huge. The guy was massive. And coming for us. Lexi pointed the gun and in that moment, I was calm. Just one guy left and we could get out of there. I don't want to say that I was happy to see this guy die. But I was. I was just so ready for all this to be over. Lexi the Glitter Queen, my former nemesis, was about to end it all.

But when no shot came and the big dude was still coming at us, I realized it wasn't over. I could see her pulling the trigger, but nothing happened. No click, no sound, just nothing. Rob wasn't crying anymore, he was smiling. This horrible smirk on his big stupid face.

"I got you now ladies. I think we're going to have some fun," the big dumb monster said.

He was right outside the DJ booth, and Lexi jumped down and tried to run, but Rob caught her by the arm. He held her with one hand while reaching for me with the other. He snagged the string on my bikini top and it pulled loose. I undid the top tie and he was left with nothing but my the skimpy bikini brat. I was topless now, but free.

I ran to the bar. I remembered the rifle that Lexi had left there. She hadn't taught me how to use it. Or maybe I just forgot. I don't know. It was lying just next to Kurt's severed head. I wish that Eric or Sid had remembered to close his damn eyes when they decapitated him. Another horrible sight I'll see in my dreams for the rest of my life.

I picked up the rifle, but almost dropped it. It was way heavier than I had expected. I could barely lift it. I wasn't sure if I could even shoot it. But I guess the adrenaline helped. At least a little bit. Trying to run from the bar back to the DJ booth carrying a big black rifle in my stripper heels was probably quite the sight.

Rob had Lexi on the floor close to where Roxy lay. Not to mention all the other bodies. Which made what he was attempting to do to her all the more disgusting. He was too dumb to figure out how to take her bra off, but was still trying. Lexi was one of the toughest chicks I've ever known, but she wasn't much of a match for this big meathead. She struggled underneath his bulk.

He was so focused on her that he didn't see me coming. I wasn't sure if there was a safety on this gun, which I'm pretty sure was an AR-15. But it could have been a modified Nerf gun for all I knew. I had it aimed at his back. Like the broad side of a barn, there was no way I could miss it. I pulled the trigger, but it wouldn't budge. Lexi was squirming and screaming. I grunted and tried again. But I got nothing. I was in a full panic. Like total freak out. I shivered from the hair on my head to my purple toenail polish. I felt like the fear might rattle me to pieces. Just one more bad guy to go, and Lexi and I would make it out of all this alive. She had saved my life and it was time to save hers.

I felt along the side of the gun and there it was, the little safety switch. I clicked it off. Rob had noticed me and lifted up off of Lexi to turn and look. He moved out of the way just as I pulled the trigger one last time. If he had only stayed still, I would have blown a hole through his spine. Instead, my bullet hit Lexi in the upper chest. She stopped struggling and went silent. And the big dumb meathead started to laugh as he was covered in her blood.

I pulled the trigger again and this time I hit him in the arm. He was knocked backward, but only for a second. His arm was bleeding, but he still managed to stand up to charge towards me. I fired again, this time missing him altogether. Bleeding and laughing, he threw himself at me.

His arm was shredded and he was losing blood fast. His knees buckled and he dropped to the floor. He still had that rotten smirk on his face, but he looked like he was bleeding out.

"Come here little lady. I got something for ya," he said, but his voice was starting to sound weak.

He probably would have died if I had just left him alone. And definitely when the bombs went off, but my anger overrode my panic. I guess I wanted revenge at that moment. I mean who wouldn't? Big Mike and his douchebags made all this happen. All my friends were dead. All because Mike got in with some crazy scientist dude to sell some designer drug. His sociopathic goons out to defend him. Seriously, *fuck* this guy.

Rob wasn't going anywhere. I dropped the rifle and took off my shoes, never taking my eyes off him. He was lying on his back and moaning, eyes closed. I hoped it hurt.

I walked up to him with that one tarnished stiletto inn my hand. The one with the worn-down heel and the metal showing through. I kneeled down next to him and he opened his eyes. I think he thought I was going to help him. *As if.*

I raised my shoe and drove the heel right into his eyeball. He screamed. And then screamed some more when I pulled it out. Some of his eyeball still on the point. He tried to swipe at me with the hand not attached to his wounded arm, but he was just flailing at that point. His big fist was easy to dodge.

I lifted my shoe again and plunged the heel into his other eye. This time going deeper. I think I hit his big stupid brain, because he finally shut up and went limp.

And that was it. I was left alone.

8

I sat there in the bloody muck for a few moments, catching my breath. My legs were shaking and tingling when I finally stood up. I might have stayed there longer if I hadn't remembered that there were likely bombs that were going to explode. Although, I didn't know if they were on a timer, or needed to be set off. I know about as much about bombs as I do guns. But I figured it would be a bad move to sit there much longer.

I thought about just leaving and calling the police. Seemed logical. But as I considered it, I didn't think that would be smart either. A stripper sitting in a strip club full of dead bodies. Some of those bodies had come to life. I mean, was I really going to try to explain that a mad scientist had infected himself with some sort of zombie virus in some crazy murder- suicide plot? The massive amount of cocaine, guns and money upstairs wasn't something I was in a hurry to talk about either. They'd toss me in a loony bin or jail. And those were the best-case scenarios. My fingerprints would be on the gun that killed Lexi too.

So that is why I did what I did. I went upstairs. Flies were crowding around Lenny's body, kind of like the zombie strippers had done when he had gotten himself trapped at the top of the pole. I tried not to look, but it wasn't easy. The safe was still standing open. There were two large blue duffle bags at the bottom of the safe and I stuffed all the cash in them. They barely closed when I was finished. Lenny's car keys were hanging on a hook nearby, and I grabbed them on my way out.

I went down to the dressing room, passing what was left of Kelly in the hallway. Inside the dressing room, Charlie was where we left him, but his eyes had popped open. I started to cry then. I rinsed the blood off of me in the little bathroom shower. Usually the girls would use it to rinse off the glitter and other vile stuff before they went home. The glitter was almost certainly transferred on to them from Lexi. That stuff is like malaria; it spreads all over the place and never quite goes away.

I threw on the T-shirt and jeans I had worn to work along with my flip-flops. I didn't take my purse or wallet. I hadn't totally thought about what I was going to do exactly, but I didn't think I was going to need my ID again. At least not that one. If the club was blown to bits like Big Mike said, I thought that if they found my ID I would just be assumed to be dead. I did grab my phone though and stuck in my back pocket, which was kind of dumb I guess. A smart phone is better ID than an ID.

I hurried out of the dressing room and passed the bar on the way out the door, but stopped. I knew I should just get out of there but something made me pause. I set down the bags and walked behind the bar. I ignored Kurt's head and went to his body. Not quite as disturbing as his head, but pretty gnarly just the same. I dug through his pockets. Not sure what I was looking for. Answers I guess. I found them, sort of.

In his right front pocket, I found a used syringe. I'm super lucky it didn't stab me. I also found a handwritten note. It read:

"If anyone ever reads this it will mean that I failed. If I'm correct, the compound I made will end humanity, as we know it. As a species, we have become a vapid sex-obsessed society of degenerates. What better place to end it all than the deviant world of the strip club? Where women take advantage of desperate men for money. Emasculating men and turning them into whiny little cucks. The vile descendants of Eve, women have destroyed everything beautiful and damned us all. I'm only returning the favor. My only hope is that God will reward me for my sacrifice and return the earth to state of paradise it was before the fall of man."

So, yeah, Kurt was a crazy piece of shit.

When I walked out of the club, it was daylight, just after 10am according to my phone. Around fourteen hours since I walked into work on a boring weeknight shift. I found Lenny's car and tossed the bags in the trunk. I opened the driver's side and was about to start the car when I remembered that I had been bit. I also remembered that I still held the note with the chemical that might have the name of the anecdote on it.

Now that I was outside, I wondered if the internet would work. I looked and saw that I had bars. I had stuffed the yellow sticky note in my pocket when I got dressed and I pulled it out.

"Neutralizer = polyethylene terephthalate"

I opened my browser and searched the word, and got the following result:

Cosmetic-grade glitter is often made from acrylic or polyester, usually polyurethane terephthalate (PET), a plastic which is non-toxic. It may or may not contain aluminum which catches light to give 'sparkle.'

I started to laugh in spite of myself. Thanks to Lexi and her insufferable glitter, I'm not going to turn into a zombie. Of all the weird and unbelievable things that happened, that may be the craziest. Lexi would have been ok too, had I not shot her. I stopped laughing and started sobbing. I sat there and cried for twenty minutes, and would have cried longer if I hadn't thought of the bombs.

I was sitting there with my stupid phone in my lap with a trunk full of cash in a car I was about to steal. The day shift crew would be coming any time, and if the bombs went off, the police would be there shortly too.

Still crying, I got up and hurried back to the club. I picked up the brick that sat by the door. They used it to prop the door open when the entry line got long on the weekend nights. I went inside put my phone on the bar and smashed it with the brick. Then I ran back outside, and hopped in Lenny's car and started the engine.

I don't even know when I stopped crying.

I barely made it out of the parking lot to the empty street before I heard the explosion.

I looked in the rearview mirror, too afraid to turn my head back, and saw that the two goons had done a thorough job with the bombs. Maybe I owe them more credit than I had been giving them. There would be nothing left but a pile of rubble. And with any luck, that pile of rubble would catch fire too.

I think I was smiling. Kurt had failed. Unless there was more of that stuff, there wouldn't be any more zombies. No one but me would ever even know what happened there.

That was all only a few hours ago. I've been driving ever since.

I stopped only to get this phone and something to eat. Although, I'm thinking this phone was a bad idea. It is now the only record of what happened. I could still go to the police, but I don't think they'd believe me if I told them the truth. Shit, I don't even know if I believe me. What if I got slipped some hallucinogen and imagined it all?

That's not true though, my ankle hurts a lot now. I'm exhausted but lucid. I could try and make up a story for the authorities, but I'm a terrible liar. No way am I passing a polygraph.

I'm pretty sure I have a few million in the trunk of this car. I'm not that far from the Mexican border, and I got enough money and Spanish to be comfortable. I didn't have many friends outside the club. I'll miss my parents, but maybe I'll find a way to contact them. So I'm going to keep driving south. I'll dump the car as soon as I cross the border. Start a new life.

I wrote a few stories in high school and always wanted to be a writer. This story could be my first. And no one will even know it's not fiction. The first thing I need to do is ditch this phone. Right after I hit stop, I'm going to wipe it clean, take it apart, and throw it piece by piece out the window.

I'm on my way to a new life, and a new me. Pretty literally, as the old me could end up a fugitive. But so many doors have been opened. And despite my throbbing ankle, that feels damn good.

Subscribe to Crystal Lake Publishing's Dark Tide series for updates, specials, behind-the-scenes content, and a special selection of bonus stories - http://eepurl.com/hKVGkr

THE END?

Not if you want to dive into more of the Dark Tide series.

Check out our amazing website and online store
or download our latest catalog here.
https://geni.us/CLPCatalog

We always have great new projects and content on the website to dive into, as well as a newsletter, behind the scenes options, social media platforms, our own dark fiction shared-world series and our very own webstore. Our webstore even has categories specifically for KU books, non-fiction, anthologies, and of course more novels and novellas.

ABOUT THE AUTHORS

Jay Wilburn was an author of horror and speculative fiction that lived in coastal South Carolina near Myrtle Beach. He taught public school for sixteen years before becoming a full-time writer. His signature series is the *Dead Song Legend Dodecology* and for younger readers, *The Lake Scatter Wood Tales*.

Armand Rosamilia is a New Jersey boy currently living in sunny Florida, where he writes when he's not sleeping. He's happily married to a woman who helps his career and is supportive, which is all he ever wanted in life . . .

He's written over 200 stories that are currently available, including crime thrillers, supernatural thrillers, horror, zombies, contemporary fiction, nonfiction and more. His goal is to write a good story and not worry about genre labels.

He also loves to talk in third person . . . because he's really that cool. Maybe.

You can find him at https://armandrosamilia.com for all of his information as well as random things he enjoys.

Erin Louis is a former adult entertainer, with a love of books, writing and humor. My job has given me a unique perspective on life. I spent twenty years as an exotic dancer on and off and started writing nonfiction as a way to shed light on a misunderstood industry and profession.

My passion for writing began with nonfiction, but I have always loved horror fiction. Stephen King, Lois Duncan, and Clive Barker got me through some tough years growing up. I found an escape through those books along with countless others. My own fiction reflects those influences as well as my love for all things dark and maybe just a bit scary.

Readers . . .

Thank you for reading *Dead Shall Rise.* We hope you enjoyed this 10th book in our Dark Tide series.

If you have a moment, please review *Dead Shall Rise* at the store where you bought it.

Help other readers by telling them why you enjoyed this book. No need to write an in-depth discussion. Even a single sentence will be greatly appreciated. Reviews go a long way to helping a book sell, and is great for an author's career. It'll also help us to continue publishing quality books. You can also share a photo of yourself holding this book with the hashtag #IGotMyCLPBook!

Thank you again for taking the time to journey with Crystal Lake Publishing.

Visit our Linktree page for a list of our social media platforms.
https://linktr.ee/CrystalLakePublishing

Our Mission Statement:

Since its founding in August 2012, Crystal Lake Publishing has quickly become one of the world's leading publishers of Dark Fiction and Horror books in print, eBook, and audio formats.

While we strive to present only the highest quality fiction and entertainment, we also endeavour to support authors along their writing journey. We offer our time and experience in non-fiction projects, as well as author mentoring and services, at competitive prices.

With several Bram Stoker Award wins and many other wins and nominations (including the HWA's Specialty Press Award), Crystal Lake Publishing puts integrity, honor, and respect at the forefront of our publishing operations.

We strive for each book and outreach program we spearhead to not only entertain and touch or comment on issues that affect our readers, but also to strengthen and support the Dark Fiction field and its authors.

Not only do we find and publish authors we believe are destined for greatness, but we strive to work with men and woman who endeavour to be decent human beings who care more for others than themselves, while still being hard working, driven, and passionate artists and storytellers.

Crystal Lake Publishing is and will always be a beacon of what passion and dedication, combined with overwhelming teamwork and respect, can accomplish. We endeavour to know each and every one of our readers, while building personal relationships with our authors, reviewers, bloggers, podcasters, bookstores, and libraries.

We will be as trustworthy, forthright, and transparent as any business can be, while also keeping most of the headaches away from our authors, since it's our job to solve the problems so they can stay in a creative mind. Which of course also means paying our authors.

We do not just publish books, we present to you worlds within your world, doors within your mind, from talented authors who sacrifice so much for a moment of your time.

There are some amazing small presses out there, and through collaboration and open forums we will continue to support other presses in the goal of helping authors and showing the world what quality small presses are capable of accomplishing. No one wins when a small press goes down, so we will always be there to support hardworking, legitimate presses and their authors. We don't see Crystal Lake as the best press out there, but we will always strive to be the best, strive to be the most interactive and grateful, and even blessed press around. No matter what happens over time, we will also take our mission very seriously while appreciating where we are and enjoying the journey.

What do we offer our authors that they can't do for themselves through self-publishing?

We are big supporters of self-publishing (especially hybrid publishing), if done with care, patience, and planning. However, not every author has the time or inclination to do market research, advertise, and set up book launch strategies. Although a lot of authors are successful in doing it all, strong small presses will always be there for the authors who just want to do what they do best: write.

What we offer is experience, industry knowledge, contacts and trust built up over years. And due to our strong brand and trusting fanbase, every Crystal Lake Publishing book comes with weight of respect. In time our fans begin to trust our judgment and will try a new author purely based on our support of said author.

With each launch we strive to fine-tune our approach, learn from our mistakes, and increase our reach. We continue to assure our authors that we're here for them and that we'll carry the weight of the launch and dealing with third parties while they focus on their strengths—be it writing, interviews, blogs, signings, etc.

We also offer several mentoring packages to authors that include knowledge and skills they can use in both traditional and self-publishing endeavours.

We look forward to launching many new careers.

This is what we believe in. What we stand for. This will be our legacy.

Welcome to Crystal Lake Publishing— Tales from the Darkest Depths.